"Release me, *now*

From her handbag Layla [...] envelope, which she exte[...] business first."

"What is that? A ransom demand?"

Her laugh was morose. "In a way."

Sebastiano stared at her in disbelief, hardly able to believe what was happening. Layla had cuffed him to the bed and it was no kinky sex game. "Have you lost your mind?"

Her smile was as morose as her laugh. "Probably. Pregnancy can do that to a woman."

For the second time in minutes his blood turned to ice.

Her shoulders rose jerkily and her face scrunched again. "I'm three months pregnant. That envelope has the scan picture in it with our baby's due date and other pertinent information."

The Diamond Club

Billion-dollar secrets behind every door...

Welcome to The Diamond Club: the world's most exclusive society, open only to the ten richest men and women alive. The suites are opulent. The service is flawless. And privacy is paramount! You'll never see the details of these billionaires' blistering romances in any of the papers—but you can read all about them right here!

Baby Worth Billions by Lynne Graham

Pregnant Princess Bride by Caitlin Crews

Greek's Forbidden Temptation by Millie Adams

Italian's Stolen Wife by Lorraine Hall

Heir Ultimatum by Michelle Smart

His Runaway Royal by Clare Connelly

Reclaimed with a Ring by Louise Fuller

Stranded and Seduced by Emmy Grayson

All available now!

HEIR ULTIMATUM

MICHELLE SMART

Harlequin

PRESENTS

ISBN-13: 978-1-335-93902-9

Heir Ultimatum

Harlequin Enterprises ULC
22 Adelaide St. West, 41st Floor
Toronto, Ontario M5H 4E3, Canada
www.Harlequin.com

Printed in Lithuania

Recycling programs for this product may not exist in your area.

MIX
Paper | Supporting responsible forestry
FSC® C021394

Michelle Smart's love affair with books started when she was a baby and would cuddle them in her cot. A voracious reader of all genres, she found her love of romance established when she stumbled across her first Harlequin book at the age of twelve. She's been reading them—and writing them—ever since. Michelle lives in Northamptonshire, England, with her husband and two young smarties.

To Laurie, thank you for being such a great support and for putting up with me xxx

CHAPTER ONE

LONDON'S SKYLINE, Sebastiano Russo grudgingly admitted, looked spectacular that evening with the soft glow of the setting sun creating a shimmering golden haze around its iconic rooftops. The helicopter he was travelling from Edinburgh in swooped down and landed on one of the most magnificent London buildings of all, the elegant home to the world's most exclusive private members' club.

As usual Lazlo, the unobtrusive manager of the Diamond Club, was there to greet him on the roof and whisk him inside.

Being in no mood for small talk and with no inclination to seek the company of the other club members in residence that evening, Sebastiano headed straight to his private suite. Losing a billion euros of his fortune in one fell swoop had a way of making a man not want company, especially when the reasons for losing said billion euros was down to your own mindlessness.

At least here he could switch the world off. The Diamond Club's facilities and services along with its innate alluring ambience gave him everything he needed when wanting to let off steam during his business trips in London. As the face of Russo Banca Internazionale, image was everything so any potentially scandalous behaviour was kept strictly behind closed doors. For centuries, the Russo family had owned and steered the glamorous private banking institution with discretion and a touch of glamour. Its high-end customers—clients had to deposit a minimum five million euros to open an account—valued the high returns paid out even during world economic turbulence and the faultless, personalised service. Since Sebastiano had taken the helm, he'd prioritised expanding its wealth management arm and enhancing its digital services without losing any of the little touches that made their clients feel so valued. Under Sebastiano's stewardship, RBI's profits had doubled in five years. If Sebastiano's loss should be made public then his reputation and his bank's reputation would be decimated. Who would trust a man to take care of their wealth if that same man couldn't take care of his own?

For this one night he would allow himself to brood in solitude. Come the morning, he would summon his core team and talk damage limitation strategies.

It had been three months since he'd last visited the Diamond Club. Three months since he'd thrown that spontaneous party in his suite which had ended in the most unexpected way. It was the longest he'd spent between visits since Raj Belanger had invited him to join the club.

There would be no partying that night. The only company Sebastiano wanted was the bottom of a bottle of bourbon and someone prepared to fade into the background pouring it for him.

Lazlo remained silent until they arrived at the double doors of Sebastiano's suite. With a respectful nod, a bow of his head and a murmured wish for Sebastiano to have a peaceful evening, he disappeared with his usual unob-trusiveness. This was one of the many things Sebastiano liked about the Diamond Club. It wasn't just that the staff were all highly trained with discretion practically em-bedded in their DNA, it was that they all had the ability to judge their guests' moods with nothing more than a look and adapt their own personas to suit what they intu-ited was wanted from them. In all his years as a member there, the staff had always intuited his mood perfectly.

Having given pre-instructions that only a bar tender was required that evening, Sebastiano shrugged off his suit jacket in the small reception area of his suite and slung it on the back of an armchair, then ripped off his tie and chucked it on the jacket. The cufflinks were the next to be removed before he headed into the suite's main living area rolling the sleeves of his shirt up, only to take one look at the bar tender and come to an abrupt halt.

A long beat passed before the willowy dark blonde woman greeted him with a respectful smile. 'Good eve-ning, Mr Russo.'

Chest tightening, eyes narrowing, he bypassed the pool table and football table that never failed to make a billionaire of any age light up like a child, and pulled up a stool at the long, dark redwood bar. 'Layla,' he ac-knowledged with a taut nod to match the tautness in his voice. 'I thought you were moving on.'

If he'd known her notice period hadn't ended, he would have made sure to notify Lazlo of his wish for a different dedicated bar tender.

The last thing he'd wanted was to be confronted by the one member of the Diamond Club's staff that he'd spent the night with.

She flashed the smile that accentuated her high cheekbones. 'Still here, just,' she confirmed lightly, in exactly the same tone with which she always served him. 'Bourbon, one cube of ice?'

He narrowed his stare again, searching her beautiful features for even a hint of reproach or peevishness but found nothing. Nothing to suggest Layla would behave with anything less than the intuitive professionalism that had led to him requesting she always serve his bar when he was in residence.

'Forget the ice,' he said gruffly, 'and make it a large one.'

Her brief smile this time was sympathetic, as if she'd peeped into his mind and seen the colossal mistake that had blighted his day and had the potential to blight the rest of his life.

She poured his drink and placed the crystal tumbler before him.

He drank it in one swallow. 'Another.'

The process was repeated. Only once he felt the liquid start to work its soothing magic did he slow his pace and sip his third glass. Rolling his taut neck, he said, 'Music. Anything of your choice but no jazz.' A cousin had once bored him for an entire Sunday afternoon with a lecture on jazz appreciation. If there was anything to appreciate about it, Roberto's monotonous, droning voice had put Sebastiano off for life.

'Something upbeat?'

Layla's musical voice could never be described as monotonous or droning, he thought, taking another large sip.

He nodded.

She tapped on a tablet and within moments rhythmic beats pulsed lowly through the vast room.

In the two years Layla had worked at the club she'd proved herself the most intuitive of all the staff to his needs and wants, and as the bourbon, helped by the music, continued to soothe the edges of his angst, the tightness in his chest that had formed at seeing her manning his bar loosened a little too.

Post-coital promises were never meant in the way real promises were, he told himself. Everyone knew that. Layla was an adult and there was nothing in her body language to suggest she was upset at his failure to call her. Now that he was a little more settled and a bit more clear in his thinking, the only impression he was receiving was that of a woman pleased to see him.

Well, it *had* been a great night that they'd shared together. The kind of night that lingered.

Relaxing even more, he raised his glass at her. 'Join me?'

Something sparkled in her forget-me-not-blue eyes. Pretty white teeth grazed the bottom lip of a wide mouth with a cupid's bow in the top lip and which three months ago had trailed kisses over every inch of his skin. 'Maybe later.'

He raised an eyebrow at the suggestiveness in her tone and the sweep of her long eyelashes.

She didn't miss a beat, arching her own eyebrows in return.

A frisson raced through his veins.

He recognised that look. It was one they'd shared three months ago in the hours before he'd thrown his guests out of the suite.

Maybe he wouldn't have to forget his troubles in a bottle or two of bourbon after all, he mused as anticipation roused. There were other, far more pleasurable ways to shake off a bad mood and if there was a pleasure greater than Layla wrapping her long legs around his waist and scraping her nails down his back while he plunged deep inside her, he was yet to experience it.

The sparkle deepened into a gleam and she leaned over the bar to top up his glass. For a moment her smart black, V-necked top gaped open, giving him a glimpse of the small, high breasts that had fitted perfectly into his mouth.

As she saw the direction of his stare, her mouth quirked in the corner. When she leaned over the bar again, this time resting her chin on her closed fist, and murmured, 'Can I get you anything else?' there was no doubt in Sebastiano's mind that the gape allowing him to see her black lace bra was deliberate.

The frisson deepened. He was close enough to smell her soft, subtle perfume, his mouth filling with the remembered taste of those perfect breasts, tongue tingling to remember the texture of her large raspberry-coloured nipples. Gazing into her eyes, he murmured back, 'Maybe later.'

Her lips widened into the lopsided smile that was her only flaw. And it wasn't even a flaw. Without it, her face would just be jaw-droppingly beautiful. Her smile turned her beauty into something spectacular. And sexy. It was a smile that promised erotic, hedonistic nights and by God had the reality matched up to the promise. To breathe in her perfume and the heat of her skin and to know that very soon those long legs could be wrapped around him again...

'How come you're still working here?' he asked after taking another long sip of his bourbon.

She gave the lightest shrug. 'My plans changed.'

'So you're staying?'

'No.' Another lopsided smile and sweep of the long lashes. 'This is my last shift.'

Now he was the one to sweep his gaze, taking another open peek at the small breasts wrapped in black lace before meeting her stare again and raising his glass. 'Then fortune is shining in my favour.'

Her elbow inched a little closer to him. 'It didn't look as though you thought fortune was on your side when you walked in here,' she observed.

Her intuition really was exceptional.

'Trust me,' he said ruefully. 'Today has been the day from hell.'

Sympathy brimmed. 'Want to talk about it?'

'No.' In his next breath he said, completely unbidden, 'I lost a billion euros.'

The Diamond Club's staff were the best in the business, from the level of service they provided, to their discretion, to showing no reaction whatsoever at any of the snippets of gossip or state secrets they became privy to in the course of their work, but even Layla's forget-me-not eyes widened at this.

He swallowed what was left in his glass and wiped his mouth with his thumb. 'Want to know how?'

Straightening, she reached for the bottle. 'Only if you want to tell me.'

What the hell? Layla had proved herself an excellent sounding board over the years. The best sounding board. What he told her went in one ear and out of the other. 'A company I'm the majority shareholder of in a personal capacity went into administration last night. On paper, I am now one billion euros poorer.'

She made an 'ouch' face and refilled his glass.

He drank with a grimace. 'I should have sold. The warning signs were there.'

After a day spent berating and raging at himself for his idiocy, he was still none the wiser as to where the lethargy in his brain that had prevented him acting on his instincts had come from. Anyone with an ounce of nous had known to sell and dissociate from a company that had turned toxic.

'I'm not used to screwing up,' he added after another drink.

'You're human,' she said softly. 'Screwing up happens to the best of us.'

'Not to me.'

She stared at him meditatively then put her elbow back on the bar and her chin back on her fist. 'Want to know what I think?'

Surprised—Layla rarely commented on the stuff he confided in her—he stared back and then shrugged. He supposed there was a slim possibility that a bar tender who doubled as a waitress was capable of an insight into his psyche that he hadn't considered. 'Sure.'

'I think you work too hard.'

'I have a lot of responsibility.' An understatement.

'I know, but when did you last take a break?' she challenged, eyeballing him in the sexiest manner imaginable.

'I take plenty of time off,' he said eyeballing her right back.

She leaned a little closer. 'I mean a proper break. A holiday, something like a trip around the Med on your yacht but without your PA, lawyer and accountant in attendance... I bet if you were to call them and order them here, they'd be knocking on the door within minutes.'

He couldn't help grinning at how on-the-nail her observation was, and was rewarded with another of her sexy lopsided smiles.

'I doubt you ever fully switch off,' she continued, her musical voice pitched low and sensuous. 'I bet you even check your emails on Christmas Day.'

'Think how much more money I'd lose if I didn't check them every day,' he riposted.

'You could afford to lose a billion euros a day for a month and still have billions left over.'

'I'd like to keep *all* my billions, not be left with scraps.'

'Then take my advice and take a break. A proper break. Recharge your batteries.' Their faces were now only inches apart. 'You know another thing that's good for stress?'

'Bourbon?'

She gave a short, soft laugh and leaned closer still. A lock of her silky hair tickled against his cheek as she whispered, 'A deep tissue massage.'

'Hmm... Now that sounds like something I'd be up for.'

'I just bet you would,' she said knowingly before another gleam lit her eyes. 'Shall I call the spa?'

He tilted his face. Their lips were a whisper away from brushing together. The sweetness of her breath filling his senses only added to the intoxication firing through his veins. Spearing his hand into the mass of thick, wavy tresses, he murmured, 'I can think of someone else I'd rather do it.'

Her lips parted against his. The sweet tongue that had explored him with the same passion as her mouth flickered against his lips but before he could mould his mouth to hers, she'd slithered back and out of reach. The hair he'd been holding fell like a waterfall around her shoulders.

Eyes full of cat-like sensuality, she gave her lopsided, oh, so sexy smile. 'I'll get some massage oil. Go and make yourself comfortable in your bedroom.'

Sebastiano stripped his clothes down to his briefs, hot blood pumping hard through him.

This was not an outcome he'd anticipated when he'd decided to end his day from hell by drowning his sorrows at his private club. The only outcome he'd anticipated was a banging hangover.

The last time his blood had pumped this hard was that night three months ago.

He'd fantasised about Layla for two years.

Her beauty had blown his mind from the first look. The tall, willowy blonde who could have graced the cover of any glossy magazine had entered his suite carrying a box of champagne for a small party he'd been hosting, and when she'd smiled at him all he'd been able to think was that there could be no sexier creature on the planet.

But she was staff. Not *his* staff, but still staff, paid to serve and cater to his every whim, part of his world but not of it. To seduce her would have been an abuse of his power. That didn't mean he couldn't request that she always tend his bar when he was in residence and enjoy feasting his eyes on her. Enjoy her company. Enjoy being able to unwind and confide things about his life with her and enjoy the sensation that she was listening because she was genuinely interested and not just because she was being paid. It helped that he doubted she retained much of what he confided.

The frisson that accompanied their talks when they were alone together was, he'd long been certain, mutual. And then she'd told him while lining up the glasses in preparation for the party he'd been throwing three months ago that it would probably be the last of his parties she worked at because she'd handed her resignation in.

The look that had flowed between them at those words...

Sebastiano's intention to party until the sun came up had been thrown out of the window, as had all his guests when midnight struck and he'd sent them home. He'd sent all the staff out too. Everyone except Layla.

There had been no doubt about what would happen the moment they were alone together. The last of the guests couldn't have left the corridor before she was locked in his arms. It had been the most thrillingly sensuous night of his thirty-five years, so thrilling that he'd taken her number and promised to call after his meeting and arrange a proper date. At the time he'd even meant it.

Which was why seeing her behind his bar had at first been such an unwelcome surprise.

Enough time had passed that he'd thought it right to assume he would never see her again and now, with anticipation burning so brightly inside him, he could barely remember why he'd changed his mind about calling her.

One more night with the woman who'd spent two years weaving through his fantasies…

He was sitting on his bed propped against the headboard wearing only his black briefs when she appeared in his open doorway holding a small bottle of massage oil.

Pressing her cheek against the door's frame, she slowly, unashamedly, swept her stare over his naked torso, all the while grazing her bottom lip with her teeth. It was enough to send the blood straight into his loins and relight his arousal.

With the face of a Hollywood siren in its golden age and the body of a supermodel, Layla wasn't hot, she was scorching and when she moved from the frame and stepped out of her heels, moisture filled his mouth.

Honey-blonde hair spilled around her shoulders, she walked seductively towards him, her short black skirt displaying her long, toned golden legs for his delectation, hips gently swaying. When she reached the foot of his bed she lightly ran her fingers over his calf.

'Turn over,' she murmured.

He obeyed, resting his cheek on a pillow. Anticipation thudded through him.

Why the hell hadn't he called her?

The light was dimmed. The mattress dipped. Air moved as she made herself comfortable beside him. The shock of cold oil poured down his spine. His flinch was automatic. Her musical laughter was soft.

It was the single most erotic moment of his life.

Her knees pressed against his side, she spread her palms and smoothed the oil over his back and shoulders, and then she got to work, kneading at his muscles with the whole of her hands, gripping the bicep closest to her and stretching his arm out so she could work her magic on his forearm too. So damn good did it all feel that if her breasts hadn't made the occasional brush against his back when she stretched herself to massage his other bicep, he might have relaxed enough to fall asleep. As it was, Sebastiano found himself caught on the cusp between pleasure and pain: the pleasure coming from her clever hands, the pain from his unrelenting arousal.

The deepening of Layla's breaths as she worked on him told Sebastiano that he wasn't the only one aroused.

Lips brushed the nape of his neck.

He groaned, would have twisted round onto his back if she hadn't pressed the tips of her fingers into his skull and kissed the rim of his ear before whispering, 'Close your eyes and don't move.'

Used to being the seducer, he found the novelty of being the seduced heightened the eroticism, heightened the thrums of desire pulsing through him.

He'd had no clue that the worst day of his life would end in such glorious eroticism. It was almost worth losing a billion euros for.

He heard a rustling beneath him but there was no time to wonder what she was doing for now she was straddling his lower back, mouth hot in the arch of his neck.

'Keep your eyes closed,' she commanded seductively. 'No moving.'

With her incredible body draped over him and the heat of her breath dancing sensation over his skin, Sebastiano had no wish to do anything but continue to obey.

Hands smoothed up his right arm. A breast covered in too many layers whispered against his cheek. He groaned again, resisting the compulsion to open his mouth and—

A shock of cold metal wrapped around his wrist. In the split second it took for him to open his eyes, Layla had leapt off him and parked herself at the foot of the bed.

It took another split second for him to register that she'd handcuffed him to the bed post.

CHAPTER TWO

LAYLA'S HEART WAS beating so hard she feared the force of it would make her sick.

She was shaking. Shaking from the desire that had welled in her during her seduction and shaking from the nerve it had taken to follow through with her plans.

She couldn't believe she'd gone through with it. The only time she'd faltered had been when Sebastiano first walked into the suite and her heart had exploded into her ribs.

Since receiving the call three hours ago that Sebastiano Russo was coming in that evening, she'd focused her mind solely on what needed to be done. The worst of it was over but the thought of what came next made her shake even harder.

'I didn't have you pegged for liking the kinky stuff,' Sebastiano said in the heavily accented Sicilian voice that shouldn't still soak into her skin like melted butter.

She'd left enough give in the handcuffs so he could twist himself round but not enough for him to slip out of the metal restraining him to the bed, and now he was lying on his back, head up against the headboard, staring at her with that lascivious gleam in his green eyes that had got her into this whole mess.

Okay, it was the whole Sebastiano Russo package that had got her into this mess. Tall, dark and handsome men were the stuff of romance novels for a reason and it turned out she was just as susceptible to their sexy promise as the next woman. And Sebastiano was incredibly sexy. She'd felt his magnetism from the first moment she'd set eyes on him.

Being five foot seven, Layla rarely had to look up to meet a man's eyes, but with Sebastiano she did, and when she locked onto them, it was a deep pool of green that captured her. That he had a chiselled face that could make a nun swoon and a lean yet muscular body to die for were secondary. It was his eyes that did it for her. His way of making her feel that she was the only woman he'd ever looked at before.

However he made her feel, she'd slept with him without any illusions as to the kind of man he was. She still didn't know what had possessed her. In all her twenty-four years, she'd been with only with one man, a long-term relationship that had ended after graduation when he'd taken a job two hundred miles from London and they'd both agreed the distance meant it would be too much work to keep the relationship going. She'd had plenty of offers since but had far too much self-respect to sleep with anyone on a first date. Once the few men she'd dated had realised they wouldn't be getting her into bed any time soon, they'd quickly moved on.

Turned out that all she'd needed for her so-called self-respect to desert her at the first opportunity was a man her hormones jumped to attention to and waved the bunting for.

Even now, even after the night they'd shared and the

weeks spent clutching her phone, her heart skipping every time it rang, her desire for Sebastiano was as unrestrained as it had been the night she'd succumbed.

She'd had no illusions before they'd made love but in the morning she'd believed him when he'd said he wanted to see her again. Maybe if she hadn't been caught in the euphoric haze of their lovemaking she would have had the sense to realise they were just words. That he didn't mean it. She would have reminded herself that for all his devastating looks and undeniable charm, Sebastiano was, at heart, a spoilt, selfish, entitled billionaire.

How she hated that he could still affect her so physically and so deeply. There had been moments when she'd been massaging the oil over his smooth back and breathing in his cologne and the heat of his skin that the ache to turn him around and fuse her mouth to his and fuse their groins together and lose herself in their passion all over again had been close to overwhelming.

That sexy, knowing anticipatory gleam in his eyes as he waited for her to make her next move was enough to liquidise her insides and she had to pull air deep into her lungs to make her body move counter to what it ached to do.

What game was she playing? Sebastiano wondered when Layla climbed off the bed. She didn't look at him until she reached the door.

The look in her eyes turned his blood to ice. 'Layla?'

There was a tremor in her voice as she said, 'Stay where you are.' Like he could actually go anywhere restrained as he was. 'I've got something to show you.'

What the hell?

'Layla?' he called after her retreating body, tugging at the restraint on his wrist, then shouted, 'Layla!'

She was gone only moments but it was enough time for him to realise the impossibility of freeing himself without a key or a chainsaw.

When she returned she was carrying a large handbag. There was nothing seductive about the graze of her teeth when her fearful eyes fell back on him.

'You need to release me,' he warned her. Whatever this game was, he no longer wanted to play it. 'Unlock this cuff.'

Her beautiful face scrunched up, eyes closing for a few beats before they snapped back open, her composure regained. 'I will. Soon.'

'Release me, *now*.'

From her handbag she produced a small brown envelope, which she extended to him. 'Business first.'

'What is that? A ransom demand?'

Her laugh was morose. 'In a way.'

He stared at her in disbelief, hardly able to believe what was happening. Layla had cuffed him to the bed and it was no kinky sex game. 'Have you lost your mind?'

Her smile was as morose as her laugh. 'Probably. Pregnancy can do that to a woman.'

For the second time in minutes his blood turned to ice.

Her shoulders rose jerkily and her face scrunched again. 'I'm three months pregnant. That envelope has the scan picture in it with our baby's due date and other pertinent information. You're good at figures. You'll be able to work back and see that the dates prove you're the father.' Her shoulders gave another jerky rise. 'Not that there's any other contender for it as you're the only man

I've been with in years, but I knew you'd want proof. I also have a letter from my midwife confirming the window of the conception date.'

Layla squeezed her eyes shut. She'd had to beg the midwife to write the letter.

She'd thought long and hard about begging Sebastiano too but ultimately this had been the only way forward that protected her and, more importantly, protected their child.

It had been two months since she'd taken the pregnancy test. She'd almost passed out from the rush of blood to her head at seeing the positive sign on the stick.

'You've chained me up just to tell me that you're pregnant?' he asked incredulously.

'No, I've cuffed you to the bed because I need money and this was the only way I figured I could get it without you dismissing me as a fantasist and kicking me out of your suite.'

It would have been different if he hadn't ghosted her. Different too, if Sebastiano were an ordinary man. They'd have been coming at things from an even playing field but there was no chance of an even playing field between a young, ordinary woman and one of the richest, most powerful men in the world. Layla knew from the bitter experience of her own father how rich men used their wealth as a tool, and her father's wealth was a fraction of Sebastiano's. Her mother had stood no chance against her father. Layla, even with all her street-smarts and legal training, stood no chance against Sebastiano.

She pulled his phone out of her bag—she'd removed it from his jacket pocket—and dropped it on the bed within his reach. 'Five million.'

He looked at his phone, looked back at her, and laughed…except it wasn't the same timbre as his usual laughter. This was a laughter that chilled.

Fear laced her spine but she shrugged it off. She was doing this for the child growing in her belly and so long as she remembered that, she could do this. She had to.

'I'm not joking and I didn't pluck that number from thin air,' she said. 'I'm having your child and, considering your vast wealth, it's only right that our child live in a decent home. London's an expensive city.' And Layla lived in what had become one of its roughest parts. Raising a child there was unthinkable. 'I've looked at properties and there's a nice four-bed in the suburbs with a big garden that would suit us perfectly. I've also factored in the cost of raising a child until the age of eighteen and then the cost of supporting their university education if that's the route they choose to take.'

He'd sat up a little straighter against the headboard and now crossed the non-cuffed arm over his chest. 'And you think that all comes to five million?' he mocked.

'No, it comes in at much less than that, but I'm also factoring in inflation and potential unforeseen emergencies. Anything that's left over when our child finishes their education will be all theirs.'

'You have such a selfless heart,' he said in that same mocking tone before flashing his perfect teeth. It was like being smiled at by a hungry shark and made her heart clatter frantically against her ribs. 'You seriously think I'm going to give you five million euros?'

'No, five million *pounds*, and if you want me to give you the key to unlock those cuffs then yes, I seriously think you're going to give it to me. In return, I've drafted a legal document stating that the five million is the extent of your financial obligations towards me and our child and that I have no recourse to come back to you asking for more. Once the money's in my account, that's it.'

'*You've* drafted it?'

'Yes, Sebastiano, *I've* drafted it.' She pulled it out of her bag, unfolded it and held it out for him to see, making sure not to get too close.

Other than his initial anger when the penny had dropped that cuffing him to the bed wasn't a sex game, he seemed to be treating the whole situation as one big joke. She'd much prefer anger. This jovial mood was unnerving simply because of the danger underlying it. Trapping Sebastiano was like trapping a big cat. Getting within arm's reach would give him the opportunity to bite. She had little doubt that when she released him he would pounce, but by then she would have the money. Any scars that followed would be worth it for her growing child's financial security.

'I've already signed it,' she added, dropping it on the bed when he made no effort to reach for it. 'A colleague witnessed it. I covered it so all they witnessed was me signing it. Once you've transferred the money, I'll leave it with you so you can sign your part too. I've also drafted a document regarding custody of our child. It makes it nice and easy for you—sole custody is mine and you are under no obligation whatsoever to have any involvement. I hope you don't sign that one because I want our child to know you and have a proper relationship with you but I understand the world you come from, and I hope you understand when you've calmed down and think about this that I'm just trying to do right by our child. All you have to do is transfer the money and then I'll let you go and you can forget all about me again and get on with your life.'

Head shaking, he laughed loudly. 'You use physical restraints to force me into giving you money, tell me you're pregnant with my child and think I'm going to let you walk out of this suite and forget about you? Were you dropped on the head as a baby?'

'I'm not a good Sicilian woman, am I? The only thing you want from me is my body.'

Sebastiano, she'd learned from the late nights in this suite when he'd confided much about his life to her, was putting off marriage for as long as he could, something that was causing consternation amongst the rest of the Russo family. They needed him to produce an heir and set it on the same path Sebastiano, his father, grandfather, great-grandfather and countless generations of other Russos had travelled, the final destination being head of Russo Banca Internazionale. The heir they were starting to get itchy about needed to be of 'good stock' from both sides. When Sebastiano married it would be to a respectable society woman, ideally Sicilian, of independent wealth who would fit in his monied lifestyle with aplomb. Love and passion were not required.

Whenever those of his trusted peers who'd already taken the marital plunge joined him at the Diamond club, it was their mistresses hanging on their arms and no one even commented on it. It was just the way things were. Wives were for duty and breeding, mistresses for fun, and everyone knew their place. Layla had heard enough snippets of conversations to know how mistresses and lovers who fell pregnant—and that was the attitude; that it was the woman whose body was entirely to blame for conception—were to be treated with suspicion, the subsequent child hidden away like a dirty little secret. Having been abandoned by her own father, Layla had no intention of letting her child be a dirty little secret, and that was if Sebastiano even acknowledged paternity. She longed for her child's sake for him to acknowledge it but had to be realistic and accept it was unlikely. Dirty little secrets were the children of mistresses, not the children of one-night stands you'd blocked all contact with.

He looked her up and down with a smug arrogance that made her fingers itch to slap off his face. 'I don't know, I've always rated the way you pour drinks.'

Hurt and loathing filling her veins like poison, Layla folded her arms across her chest. 'You only requested that I tend your bar because you like to look at me.' Long, lingering looks that had made her all hot and fizzy inside. 'If I looked like a goblin you would never have given me a second glance, now transfer the money.'

'It's Friday evening.'

'And? Personal transfers can be made at any time.'

'I can't just transfer five million euros in one sitting. There are procedures.'

'Sebastiano, you own your own bank. You, personally, dragged it into the digital age. I *know* you can transfer the money so that it hits my account immediately, so do it because, I promise you, you won't be leaving that bed until it's done. And it's five million *pounds*.'

The satisfaction at Sebastiano's latest flash of incredulity was almost worth the danger that came with cuffing one of the richest men in the world to a bed and demanding money from him. Layla had long suspected his assumption that because she had a pretty face and worked in a role of subservience, it meant she didn't have two brain cells to rub together. Having it confirmed carried a bitter tinge though, more proof that he thought nothing of her other than as a body he desired. What lay between her ears was dismissed. Arrogant and spoilt he might be but, over the last two years, Layla had grown to like him as more than just sex on legs. She'd grown to like *him*.

Sebastiano had always thought Layla the most chameleon-like of all the Diamond Club staff but this was a side to her he would never have guessed she possessed. For two years she'd played the role of attentive bar tender to him with barely a hint to her lurking intelligence. He happily admitted to himself that this was a side to her he found *very* sexy. As incredible as it was to believe, the whole situation was sexy.

But she couldn't seriously think she would get away with this?

'Aren't you worried about the repercussions?'

She pulled a face. 'If you want to call the police and tell them the great Sebastiano Russo was arrogant enough to think a woman he'd bedded and then ghosted would willingly go to bed with him again and that he was arrogant enough to fall into her trap then be my guest. You won't have a shred of evidence to support your allegations and I'll deny everything.'

'I never said anything about involving the police,' he refuted silkily. 'I prefer to deal with situations in my own way, and it wasn't arrogance that made me think you wanted me again, it was experience. You might have seduced me for revenge and monetary gain but I know damn well that you were as turned on when giving me that massage as I was.' And he would use her desire to his advantage when he took his revenge. Already a multitude of scenarios were percolating in his head.

Colour flamed her cheeks but she didn't back down. 'If you think I still want you then I have to question whether *you* were dropped on your head.'

He flared his nostrils. 'I can still smell your arousal, *cara.*'

Skin still aflame, she tightened her folded arms. 'Stop with the mind games. None of this is for me, it's for our child, so transfer the money because I'm getting sick of your procrastination.'

He pretended to consider it. As if there were a child! They'd used protection! This was one elaborate hoax by a woman he'd scorned and severely underestimated.

She sighed into the silence. 'Okay, if you won't give me the money for our child…' She shook her head, the expression on her beautiful face morphing into one of deep regret. 'It would be a real shame if the press were tipped off that the owner of the famed international banking group Russo Banca was so careless with his own money that he lost a billion euros overnight on an investment he knew was going bad. Imagine what that would do to your reputation. Imagine what your fellow billionaires who entrust their wealth with you would think if they learned you can't be trusted to manage your own wealth.'

Layla had no idea where this threat had come from—it had reeled off her tongue before her brain could catch up and stop it—and was having to fight hard to stop the fear gripping her heart from showing on her face.

This was going way too far and now she was digging

herself a massive hole by antagonising and threatening him. Baiting the big cat that was already biding its time to pounce and sink its teeth into her neck was the height of idiocy.

None of this was going how she'd envisaged. Call her naive but she'd talked herself into believing Sebastiano would take one look at the scan picture of their baby and immediately transfer the money just to get rid of her. He'd made it patently clear he wanted nothing more to do with her. She was a warm body to him, nothing else.

Once she'd accepted she was pregnant, she'd bitten the bullet and dialled his number. She'd dialled into fresh air. He'd either blocked her or got rid of his phone. A text message that failed to deliver proved it was the former. He'd blocked her.

Trying to get hold of him through his bank had been a nightmare of comic proportions. It had taken a week of near-constant calls and emails before she reached the heady heights of his personal office. She'd left numerous messages for him to call her. At her wits' end, she'd gone as far as to tell a snooty woman that she needed to speak to Sebastiano because she was pregnant with his child. The woman had sighed and said in the most condescending voice imaginable that this was a business line and any calls of a personal nature should be made to Mr Russo's personal phone, and that if she called the business number again a restraining order would be sought, before hanging up on her.

Terrified, knowing that to hack the Diamond Club's computer system to get Sebastiano's personal details was not only impossible but that to even attempt it would end in her imprisonment, Layla knew she had to keep her employment at the club going until he made his next visit there, and so had called Lazlo asking if she could extend her notice period. As the Diamond Club's recruitment procedure was intricate and lengthy—all staff were vetted so heavily they made the security services seem lax—he still hadn't found a replacement for her and had been happy to agree.

All she had to do was wait.

And wait.

And wait.

Before their night together, Sebastiano had been a regular visitor, gracing the club at least once a month. Since that night, so much time had passed without his presence that whispers circulated amongst the staff that he was going to resign his membership.

Layla couldn't even contemplate that happening. She *had* to believe he would show again.

In the weeks and weeks of waiting, her plans on how to tell him had shifted like sand, but it wasn't until the scan the week before that the route she had to take had solidified in her mind. It was listening to her baby's heartbeat that had done it. The clutch of her own heart followed by the explosion that had rippled into every cell in her body, an explosion of love that had turned Layla into a big cat herself whose only purpose in life was to protect her unborn child.

Sebastiano would never accept her child. Her child would be worse than a dirty secret to him. He didn't want Layla. Even with proof he would likely disbelieve her and throw her out of his suite and probably out of the entire club too, and she would be left to raise a child in a part of London only the foolish or desperate ventured into at night. And so she'd brought the handcuffs. Just to stop him from throwing her out. To force him to give her the money she needed before he hid himself in a cloak of expensive lawyers like her own father had done twenty-four years ago.

Darkness flashed in the green pools holding her gaze before he gave another chilling smile. 'You signed a watertight confidentiality agreement, Layla. Break it and you won't just lose the money you're blackmailing out of me. I will personally see that you lose everything.'

As frightened as she was, she'd dug this hole and now she had no choice but to stand in it and hold her nerve. 'I can't be the only person who knows about the loss so you'd have to prove that it was me who tipped the press off. You must know that journalists always protect their sources.'

'Everyone has a price,' he said sardonically.

'And mine is five million pounds. For you, that's loose change.'

The smile back on his face, he contemplated her lazily for a few nerve-wracking moments too long then gave a brisk nod of his head and stretched his uncuffed hand for his phone. 'I can see you will not accept no as an answer so let's get this done.'

CHAPTER THREE

'YOUR BANK DETAILS,' Sebastiano commanded once he'd opened his banking app.

She recited the sort code and account number off the top of her head.

'And your surname?'

Her forget-me-not eyes flashed. 'Sansom.'

He tapped it in, uncertain why he would feel disconcertment for not knowing this. There had been no need for him to know Layla's surname before. It was good that he knew it now though. It would make it easier to track her down when the time came to take his revenge. He didn't want to involve Raj or the staff here at the Diamond Club. This was between him and Layla, no one else.

Being Sicilian, revenge came as naturally to him as loving his family. Unlike the majority of his compatriots though, Sebastiano was of the opinion that revenge was better served cold. In truth, he'd had little need to act out in vengeance before. He came from an enormously wealthy, respected family. Slights of the kind that required vengeance were few and far between. When issues that angered or irritated him arose he dealt with them immediately, time being too short to waste on fools or incompetents.

Layla was neither a fool nor an incompetent. For two years she'd played him like the finest violin and tonight was her virtuoso performance.

She would realise in his own time what a mistake she'd made targeting him for that performance.

His revenge would take a much different flavour from the media's portrayal of Sicilian vengeance.

Confirmation of the transfer flashed on his screen. He held it up for her. 'Done.'

Not looking at him, she swiped at her phone, read what was on the screen and took a visible breath of relief.

Enjoy the relief. Enjoy those breaths. Soon, you will be begging to breathe easy. 'You won't get away with this. You know that, right?'

She seemed to shrink before lifting her chin and bravely saying, 'If you hurt me, you hurt our baby.'

He laughed, enjoying how the sound of his laughter made her shrink into herself again. 'I *will* hurt you, Layla, but you can sleep safe—I was raised to never lift a hand to a woman and I'm not going to start with a hustler like you. There is no baby. I applaud you on a job well done. Go and spend your ill-gotten money while you can.'

She dropped her stare. Hands shaking, she put her phone into her bag and then unzipped a pocket in it and produced a small key. Fixing her eyes back on him, she grazed so hard on her bottom lip that when she spoke he could see the indentation made by her teeth.

'I *am* pregnant, Sebastiano. I didn't want it to be like this but you ghosted me and made it impossible for me to contact you. I am giving you a way out. I *do* want you to be involved in our child's life but if you can't commit to that then please, for our baby's sake, leave me alone.'

He shook his head with faux disappointment. 'As deeply touching as that little speech was, it is time for you to release me.'

Backing away from him, she threw the key but her aim was off and it landed on the floor beside his bed on the other side from the post he was chained to.

Seeing the uncertainty cloud her beautiful face, he raised his eyebrows. 'I can't reach it, *cara*.'

The uncertainty deepened.

'I fulfilled my side of your demands,' he pointed out. 'Time to fulfil yours.'

She gave the slightest nod before tentatively moving to the side of the bed and bending down to scoop the key up.

Sebastiano waited until precisely the right moment to pounce.

Layla had never truly appreciated Sebastiano's agility or the wingspan of his muscular arms, not until she was straightening with the key in her hand and a much larger hand suddenly whipped through the air and clasped her wrist. Caught off guard, the key dropped onto the mattress as she was half pulled and half stumbled onto the bed. In the blink of an eye she found herself sprawled on top of him, her breasts crushed against his hard chest and her face in his neck, only the tips of her toes still making any contact with the thick carpet.

She was winded more through shock at the unexpected than anything physical, long stunned beats passing before she found anything approaching sense and tried to scramble off him. Tried because the arm of the hand that had captured her wrist was now wrapped around her back, trapping her to him. Trapping her against Sebastiano's mostly naked body…

Panic shot through her and she dug her hands into the mattress for the purchase needed to lift her face out of his neck then wriggled urgently…except the way she instinctively twisted to pull her face away to stop herself breathing in his scent meant she was trying to escape to the opposite side of the bed from where her feet were. Before she could demand he let her go, Sebastiano clasped her bottom and shifted beneath her, pulling her further onto the bed so she was no longer on top of him but facing him with her head in the crook of his chained arm and her legs draped over his thighs.

His gleaming green eyes captured hers. A seductive, knowing smile tugged on lips that were so close she could feel the warmth of his breath on her mouth.

It was no longer an effort to hold her breath. Layla's lungs had closed up, and when he slid his hand under her top and over her bare skin, the sensation that followed was so intense that the ache between her legs, a dull burn since she'd tortured herself by touching him so intimately, deepened into a painful throb.

This was why she'd succumbed to her desires and given herself to him. The intensity of her feelings. The depth of her desire. Lust like she'd never imagined existed, growing with each of his visits to the club, deepening with each lock of their eyes until she'd found herself fantasising about him strolling into his suite, taking one look at her and throwing her over his shoulders and carrying her to this very bed and doing whatever he wanted to her. When she'd handed her notice in, she'd known her resignation meant the unspoken, invisible physical barrier they had both erected would be torn down.

One night. That was all she'd wanted, all she'd thought she needed. But it hadn't been enough, not for either of them. The reality of their lovemaking had been headier than even her wildest fantasies. Only Sebastiano's meeting with the Bank of England the next morning had compelled them to drag themselves out of bed to shower and dress, and even then they didn't make it out of the bedroom before he had her back up against the wall.

'*Dio*, how am I going to get my head straight to discuss regulations when I can still taste your sex on my tongue?' he'd murmured, spearing her hair as he kissed her deeply. 'I will call you later, as soon as I'm free.'

But the call had never come. She'd waited until the next evening and sent him a breezy message that in no way matched the dread that had been thumping in her heart. *Hope your meeting went well and all's okay. Layla.* Blue ticks indicated the message had been delivered and read. His blocking of her had come later. She didn't know when. She didn't reach out to him again until after the pregnancy test.

She'd been so wrong. One night *had* been enough for him. He'd only responded to her seduction tonight because he was so highly sexed he would respond to any woman offering herself on a plate to him, and it was with that thought shouting in her brain that Layla clamped her lips together to swallow the moisture filling her mouth and tried desperately to tune out the pleas of her delirious body.

'Don't even think about it,' she said in a voice that was far huskier than she'd been aiming for.

Another knowing smile on his lips, he inched his face even closer. 'Think about what?'

If Sebastiano was agile he had nothing on Layla. Now she had her wits about her, she used her natural litheness to spring herself free. Feet connecting to the floor, she snatched up her handbag and raced to the door.

His mocking laughter hurt her ears. 'Run, little rabbit, run. Run as fast as you can and as far as you can. It doesn't matter. You know I will catch you.'

Sebastiano climbed out of the car and gazed up at the office block that had once been modern but now showed severe signs of wear and tear. Set in the stonework of the doorway, an intercom with a list of the businesses that occupied it. He pressed the button for Clayton Community Law and announced himself. The door buzzed. He was expected.

With a paper sign on the aged elevator declaring it out of order, he climbed the stairs to the third floor where Laurence Clayton, the law firm's bushy-white-bearded founder, was waiting in a rundown reception area for him.

'A pleasure to meet you. Thank you for agreeing to meet me out of business hours,' Sebastiano said as they shook hands.

'Believe me, the pleasure is all mine. My office is this way. Forgive the carpet. We keep hoping to replace it but funds never stretch that far.'

The threadbare carpet, Sebastiano was certain, was older than his father.

'I am quite sure we can do something about that,' he assured the man who'd set up a not-for-profit law firm three decades ago and dedicated his working life to providing free legal services for people who couldn't afford it, all paid for through fundraisers and charitable donations. 'I understand your computer system is in need of updating too?'

Laurence opened a door to reveal a small office heaped with legal texts and mountains of paperwork, and pulled a rueful face. 'Sending attachments to the courts and barristers is our biggest problem. The system is so dilapidated and cranky it can't always cope with the size of the files. We manage—we always manage—but it's frustrating because it's sucking time that should be spent helping our clients.'

Sebastiano took the offered hard chair and smiled.

Layla dragged herself out of bed after yet another fitful excuse for sleep, showered, dried her hair, and dressed carefully in skinny black trousers, a cream and black horizontally striped top, and a pair of black ankle boots that were on the cusp between funky and professional. After throwing a slice of toast and a cup of tea down her throat she went out into the cosy back garden to say goodbye to her mum.

Jilly Sansom was on her knees doing some early morning weeding, although that was really the wrong word to use for her mother's method of pulling out unwanted plants considering she found so many of them to be pretty that she tended to let them stay rooted and do as they pleased. Whatever her methods, the results were incredible, their back garden a tranquil oasis that blazed with year-round colour.

It was the garden that was making her mum prove so

stubborn about moving to the suburbs with her. The garden was her labour of love. The cannabis farm next door and their area's recent crime rate explosion paled into insignificance in her mum's mind. Layla had fallen in love with one of the houses she'd viewed that weekend, one that had a garden she was certain her mum would love, and had already arranged a second viewing to drag her mum along to. She couldn't bear to leave her behind.

Jilly beamed to see her daughter. 'You look great. Very professional.'

Layla yawned through a smile.

Eyes so like her own brimmed with compassion. 'Another bad night?'

She gave a 'what can you do?' shrug. 'It'll get better.'

'It always does,' her mum agreed then brightened again. 'Got your passport?'

'In my handbag.' She was flying to Italy that morning to meet with a mega-rich philanthropist who wanted to set up a charitable legal firm using a similar model to the one she worked for with hints of a sizeable donation to their own firm dangling before them.

She'd been blown away at being chosen to represent the company. 'Me?' she'd said on Friday to Laurence, the firm's founder, when told about it. 'But I only qualified five minutes ago!' Well, three months ago. Three months since Layla Sansom had become a fully qualified solicitor of law.

'And that's why it has to be you,' Laurence had told her earnestly. 'You could have joined any law firm when you graduated but you chose us. I'm well aware that numerous other firms have tried to poach you since you gained your full qualifications but you have stayed loyal.'

'Only because I believe in what we do.'

'And that's why it has to be you—you are still passionate about what we do.' He'd pulled a wry face. 'You haven't been around long enough to get jaded.'

'Oh, I'm sure it'll happen at some point,' she'd assured him.

He'd laughed. 'That's the spirit. But seriously, if anyone can sell the importance of our work, it's you, so clear your diary for Monday.'

After kissing her mother goodbye and promising to let her know when she'd landed, Layla went back inside, grabbed her smart black fitted jacket and carried it to the living room to wait for the car that would be taking her to the airport.

Standing at the reinforced sash bay window, she watched a small gang of teenagers in school uniform trundle to the bus stop she would normally catch her own bus to work from. Most of them were kids she'd known since they were in their own mothers' bellies, some she'd babysat for in her own teenage years. She loved the lot of them, pains in the butt that they were, but wished every interaction with them didn't come with the argument of why she wasn't going to buy cigarettes or booze for them or why she didn't want to buy cannabis from them. Poor kids. She could only pray that they stayed strong, focused on their education, and got the hell out of this neighbourhood. Pray, too, that they stayed within the walls of their homes when the sun went down. The people who roamed these streets at night were not the kind of people you looked in the eye. At night you only left your home if you had to, and if you did have to, you kept your head down and walked as fast as you could.

A tall, dark-haired man appeared on the other side of the street. Layla's heart caught in her throat and she shrank back from the window even though her brain had already registered that it wasn't him.

It had been over two weeks since she'd fled the Diamond Club. For the first week she'd shied away from all shadows. For the first week she'd behaved like a fugitive in a film, constantly looking over her shoulder and watching out for places and spaces where someone could hide and pounce. A cricked neck had stopped the constant checking over the shoulder but even now, travelling on a crowded bus through London's rush hour, she felt exposed, which was ridiculous. As if Sebastiano would be seen dead on public transport! All the same, she felt safer on busses than the tube so that was now her favoured mode of transport. She'd also taken the precaution of adding even more locks and chains to the front and back doors at home leading her mum to complain that it took longer to lock up than to brush her teeth. Although she knew deep down that these precautionary measures were a complete waste of time when up against a man with unlimited resources, they at least allowed her to get a little sleep, if not the full night she so craved.

What was even more ridiculous was that she knew perfectly well Sebastiano wasn't going to break into her home and kidnap her from her bed and he wasn't going to snatch her from the street or drag her from a bus.

Constantly thinking and worrying about the form his revenge would take was what was stopping her from sleeping. She hoped he waited a few months longer, when hopefully the pregnancy would be visible. He wouldn't be able to deny it then. Three and a half months gone and no one would guess she had a baby growing inside her.

She wished she could stop the idle fantasies that kept creeping on her when her brain became especially woolly with lack of sleep, of Sebastiano approaching her and then stopping mid-step, his gaze dipping to her stomach and the expression on his face changing from whatever revenge looked like to rapture.

Despite everything, she wanted him to want their baby. She wanted him to love it. She wanted her child to have what she'd never had—a father.

An email from a client pinged, an impoverished woman with three small children, under threat of eviction for non-payment of rent after the children's father stopped his maintenance payments. It was for people like this client that Layla had chosen her career path, people who needed but couldn't afford decent legal representation. People like her mother.

It was as she was sending her reply of reassurance that everything was in hand that a huge car with darkened windows expertly pulled in to the small gap at the front of her house. Every person within Layla's eye line turned to gawp at it.

Only when she'd unlocked all the locks and chains on the front door and stepped outside did she realise the car was a stretched Bentley.

'Wow,' she murmured. Her years at the Diamond Club had taught her more about the societal value of cars than she could ever hope to forget, and this car was of a breed of the super-rich.

The waiting chauffeur opened the back door for her. The interior was every bit as luxurious as she could have imagined, the cream seats made of the softest leather, all the panelling a highly buffed dark wood.

'If you open the panel in front of you, you will find cold drinks to help yourself to,' the chauffeur said via an intercom.

London's streets were heaving that busy Monday morning, and as they crawled their way through rush hour traffic, Layla had a marvellous time exploring the luxurious cabin. Such a marvellous time did she have that it wasn't until The Shard suddenly loomed in her vision that she realised she was being driven in completely the wrong direction for the airport...

Just as she was processing this, the driver entered an underground car park. A trickle of unease crawled up her spine.

The car came to a stop. The back door opened. A tall figure in a dark grey suit slid in.

'Hello, little rabbit.'

A handcuff was locked around her wrist before she even found the wits to scream.

CHAPTER FOUR

IT TOOK LAYLA approximately three seconds to regain her wits and understand that she'd guilelessly walked into Sebastiano's trap and that she was handcuffed to him. Three seconds for the instinct to escape to kick in, an instinct she knew would prove futile even as she yanked on the unyielding door handle and stabbed at the unresponsive window button, and shouted for the driver to let her out.

'He can't hear you,' Sebastiano said mildly as they drove up the ramp and back into the daylight.

Furious, Layla turned her head so she could glare directly at him, and, for the first time since she'd fled the bedroom of the suite she'd chained him in, made eye contact with the father of her baby. Her already wildly thumping heart accelerated.

He winked. 'Great to see you, Layla.'

Trying hard to catch a breath, a feat made harder as every snatch came with a dollop of his gorgeous cologne, she stared at his perfect face and debated which part of it she should punch.

She should have known. Potential benefactors didn't appear from nowhere. Their law firm wasn't fashionable enough to attract them without a lot of groundwork and pleading. Their clients were the kind of people who slipped under the radar of people's attention, mostly ordinary people without a tragic backstory who'd fallen on desperately hard times and had nowhere else to turn for help. Layla had started at Clayton's straight from university. The salary offered was so far below the market rate that she was the first graduate to approach them as a first resort and not a last. She hadn't cared about the money, and in any case the money from her part-time evening job at the Diamond Club had made up for it. The day she'd received her practising certificate, she'd received a modest pay rise to reflect that she was now a fully qualified solicitor, just enough extra money to enable her to quit the club.

Quit the club and sleep with its sexiest member.

As perverse as she knew it was to be feeling it, the primary emotion jostling for space with her fury was relief that the worst had finally happened. No more looking over her shoulder. Like watching a horror film, anticipation of the screams was always worse than the screams themselves. Whatever form Sebastiano's revenge took, it couldn't be worse than her imaginings, which had ranged from being thrown in the boot of a car and driven over every speed bump in England to Sebastiano using the cuffs currently binding her to him for an entirely different purpose that shouldn't have made her feel all hot and sticky just to think of it...

'Where are you taking me?' she asked tersely.

'Sicily.'

That made her back straighten. 'You are out of your mind.'

'Possibly. Being chained to a bed and blackmailed out

of five million pounds has a way of making a man...' he widened his eyes and wiggled his fingers '...a little crazy.'

'Unhinged is the word that springs to mind if you think you can kidnap me and take me out of the country.'

'I've already kidnapped you, *cara*. You've got your passport. Getting you out of the country is the easy part.'

She snorted her derision. 'And what are you planning to do if your depraved little fantasy...delusion...of getting me to Sicily works? Lock me in a dungeon?'

His eyes gleamed. 'Now that's an idea I could run with.' He lifted the wrist chained to hers, forcing her own arm to rise. 'I already have the restraints: thank you for leaving them with me. Let us hope I don't misplace the key.'

'I can look after it if you want?'

He leaned his face into hers. 'Nice try.'

Hating the pulsing sensation in her pelvis at his closeness, close enough now that every inhalation came with the musky scent of his skin as well as the cologne covering it, she gave a sarcastic smile. 'I thought so. But if you really are planning to smuggle me onto an aeroplane then there's the little matter of security and all those pesky metal detectors to get past.'

The tip of his nose a whisker from brushing against hers, his smile made her think again of the caged big cat, except this time the cat had been freed and was selecting the choicest area to take his first hungry bite. His voice dropped to a seductive whisper. 'I am confident that you will walk willingly onto my plane, no restraints required...unless requested.'

She had to expel the breath she'd been holding to ask, 'Does Laurence know what you're doing?'

He shifted back. 'Laurence believes I am your secret lover.'

Sebastiano delighted to see the multitude of expressions that flittered over Layla's beautiful face. He was quite sure she was thinking of ways to overpower and possibly maim him. His veins buzzed just to imagine her acting out those thoughts.

It was rather incredible to think that in the weeks since being chained to a bed and blackmailed out of a substantial amount of money, he'd felt more alive than he'd ever done before.

He would never have described his life as being boring or predictable but being outwitted by the bar tender he'd bedded after two years of mild flirtation had pumped him with an adrenaline that even a hard workout in his gym couldn't match. Whereas after their night together he'd ruthlessly forbidden himself from thinking about her, since her blackmail he'd luxuriated in his plans for vengeance, the image of Layla's perfect oval face, cute nose, striking eyes and lopsided smile always there whether his eyes were open or shut.

He settled back as far as their locked cuffs would allow so he could take the whole of her in. *Dio*, she was stunning even with minimal makeup, her honey-blonde hair loose and tumbling around her shoulders accentuating her high cheekbones. Her top had slipped a little, exposing a little of her smooth shoulder. Exposing, too, the strap of her blue bra, and he idly wondered if she was wearing matching panties. 'I would feel bad about lying to him but then I learned he mentored you.' Noticing her clenched fists, he smiled sympathetically.

'Don't worry, no Laurences were hurt in the planning of my vengeance.'

Layla squeezed her eyes shut in a futile attempt to quell the rage boiling in her before flashing her fury back at him. 'You had no right dragging him into this. He's a lovely man who's spent his whole life doing his best to help others. He'll be horrified when he learns you've tricked him.' Laurence was the closest thing to a father she'd ever had, the reason she hadn't doubted for a second the validity of a trip to Italy to meet a wealthy philanthropist.

'He'll only learn the truth if you tell him, and what would you have preferred? That I used your mother to get to you?'

The mention of her mother made her chest tighten.

'I did consider it,' he mused. 'But then I paid a visit to the coffee shop she works at and...'

She almost sprang off the seat in shock. 'You stalked my *mother*?'

The musing expression on his face deepened. 'I wouldn't call it stalking, more scoping the enemy.'

'You *pig*.'

'Pigs are highly intelligent creatures and far more hygienic than we give them credit for, so thank you for the compliment.'

'My mother's no one's enemy.'

'Having met her, I understand what you mean. A beautiful woman. She could be your less shouty older sister.'

If Layla's left wrist hadn't been cuffed to Sebastiano's right wrist, she'd have swung her arm into his stomach with all her furious strength. The way the bastard was relishing every moment meant he'd probably enjoy it.

'How did she take the news that she's going to be a grandmother at the tender age of forty-four?'

It took a moment to fully understand what he'd said. 'You've investigated her?'

'Not personally. How did she take the news about the "baby"?'

'What do you mean, *not personally*?'

'I mean I employed others to do the investigating, and before you ask, yes, I had everyone with a close connection to you investigated, so now you can answer my question of how she took the news about the "baby". I am assuming you told her?'

'Of course I told her—she's my mother,' she snapped. 'And she took it much better than you did.'

'So you are still sticking to the pregnancy story then?'

'Does that mean you're still in denial?'

He laughed. '*Cara*, we both know there was no conception. Not with me. You slept with me, returned to that unsavoury street you live on—yes, I paid a little visit to it—and realised I could be your ticket out of there.'

Initially, Sebastiano had been convinced Layla had planned everything, from their initial wild coupling to the blackmail. Everything he'd learned from his investigation into her had changed his mind.

When he'd first read the full report, he'd been stunned.

He'd been unaware that in all the time he'd known her, Layla had been working for a law firm gaining the experience and qualifications needed to become a solicitor in her own right, a discovery he'd found as disconcerting as when he'd heard her surname for the first time. He'd shaken the disconcertment off, telling himself there was no reason he should have known that about her. He'd shaken off the greater disconcertment that her law firm was an entirely charitable organisation with the lowest wages for solicitors in the whole of the English capital. After all, he'd reasoned, history was littered with seemingly good people burdened with dark secrets. No one was entirely pure.

Layla's resignation from the Diamond Club coincided with her qualifying as a solicitor, which suggested her blackmail had been opportunistic rather than planned. Seeing where she lived had only reinforced this notion.

'Do you really think I would choose a man like you to be my meal ticket?' she asked with incredulous heat. 'Deny it to yourself all you want but I *am*...'

He placed a finger firmly to her lips. 'No more baby talk, and no more Medusa looks at me. You have five million in your bank account and once we are married, I will transfer the same amount into your firm's account. One night of work will have earned you ten million pounds, so I think it is time you started showing me some gratitude.'

The shock on her face at this was as delicious as his chef's deconstructed tiramisu. He assumed it was this same shock that made her snatch hold of his finger and move it from her mouth rather than bite it off.

'What did you just say?' she whispered.

'Many things, but I assume it was the bit about marriage that you're referring to?'

Her eyes had widened so much they'd become perfect orbs. 'You really have lost your mind.'

'I have never felt saner or seen a clearer path in front of me.' To his surprise, he realised they'd just turned into the airport's dedicated area for private flyers. He hadn't noticed they'd cleared the throng of traffic. 'You and I will marry on Saturday, and you will use your excellent acting skills to put on an act of complete adoration otherwise I will not just destroy your life but I will personally see that Laurence and your entire law firm is destroyed too.' The only one he would spare was her mother.

The car came to a stop.

Sebastiano extracted his finger from Layla's tight grip and removed the key for the handcuffs from his jacket pocket and unlocked them. Freed, he rubbed his hands together and smiled at her. *Dio*, he was enjoying this. He'd known revenge would taste sweet but this tasted sweeter than a strawberry at the height of a British summer. 'It is now time for me to board my flight. You do not have to come with me. I will not force you onto the plane.' He leaned again into her ashen face and widened his smile. 'You are most welcome to take your chances and hope that I am bluffing.'

Layla parked herself on the luxurious soft leather seat facing Sebastiano.

'Strap yourself in, *cara*,' he said with the mocking tone she was coming to hate as much as she hated him. 'And that is no way to look at your fiancé. Think *complete adoration*.'

She shook her head in part fury and part bewilderment. She'd wanted to call his bluff, had had to force her feet to move one in front of the other up the steps and onto the plane. It had been the steeliness in his stare that had convinced her he wasn't bluffing. Oh, not about the marriage part—that was plainly bonkers—but about his intention to destroy her law firm if she didn't comply.

Her fury wasn't just directed at him either. A large portion of it was aimed firmly at herself for thinking she could take on Sebastiano Russo and escape with only minor injuries. For believing that, deep down, he was one of the good guys. For the longing that just wouldn't quit that he would accept the pregnancy and want to be a father. For the longing that just wouldn't quit for *him*.

Lifting her chin, she looked him square in the eye. 'What are you really planning to do to me?'

His hateful green eyes gleamed. 'Are you thinking dungeons again?'

She was close to being angry enough to cry. 'Stop it.'

'I can turn a section of my cellar into one that we can use as a play room if you want.' The gleam deepened. 'We can take it in turns to be restrained.'

The plane began to move.

Unable to look at him a moment longer, Layla stared out of the window beside her head.

'We are to be married in my private chapel at two o'clock on Saturday afternoon. All the wheels to make this happen have already been greased.'

The thumps of her heart were making it hard to hear clearly but every word penetrated. It was the lack of mockery in his voice that turned the thumps into thunder rolls that whooshed hot blood in her head and made her feel faint.

The plane lifted into the sky and the only word she could pull from her lips was, 'Why?'

'Because I need a wife.' There was a slight pause. 'Maybe not a wife, but I need a public distraction. Remember that billion-euro loss I told you about? You must do because it's the billion-euro loss you used to extort five million pounds from me. A journalist from a respected financial newspaper has been investigating it. My legal team are now out of legal avenues to prohibit publication. The temporary injunction lifts tomorrow morning. The journalist will publish immediately. As soon as the news is released, I will release my own statement announcing my wedding to a respectable English family lawyer. It is a tactic commonly known as burying bad news, and what better way to bury bad news that could bring down my whole company than with the wedding of the century? My network has dropped subtle hints to world and business leaders that Saturday is a day they should clear any plans made. Personalised invitations will be hand-delivered to them within an hour of the announcement.'

She couldn't stop her face from turning back to him but was reeling too much to even pull one word out, never mind string a coherent sentence together.

Perfectly understanding her expression, Sebastiano pulled a sympathetic face. 'It is a lot to take in for you.'

'But *why*?' She shook her head, trying desperately to clear the blood from it. 'I can just about get my head around the marriage aspect… Sebastiano Russo getting married will make the news, that's for sure, but how you can be sure it will bury the loss beats me and I really don't get why you would want to marry me—sure, as vengeance for what you think I've done to you it makes a form of sense in a slightly psychotic way, but I'm not a society woman like you're supposed to marry and I'm—'

'You're the best thing at short notice,' he cut in. 'You are unknown in my world, which will only add to the interest. The main criterion for a wife for a man in my position is respectability and on paper you have that. You're a lawyer. That you were abandoned before birth by your father and raised solely by your mother only gives people more to admire about you because it suggests someone who is hard-working and focused.'

She had to grip the handrails to stop herself from swaying. To hear her father's abandonment thrown so casually into the conversation almost as a weapon against herself cut to the bone. Coming from the father of the life growing inside her sent the knife to the marrow.

'My investigative team looked into your entire background,' he continued. 'You have never put a foot wrong. Only I know that behind your respectable facade lies a conniving opportunist. We will marry for a short period, until any kick back from the loss has passed, and then we will announce our separation. I can already see it: *Unfortunately, with our individual work commitments, we were unable to make our marriage work but we part ways with an abundance of love and respect for each other...* I have assured Laurence you will be back in the office in a month. When that happens, we can both embrace the workaholic lifestyles that can destroy even the closest of marriages.

Her laughter had a slight tinge of hysteria to it. 'Love and respect? Now I've heard everything.'

'I have the greatest respect for you as an adversary, *cara*. It is what will make our marriage so interesting, do you not agree?'

'What, you *want* a wife who hates you?'

A frisson of desire fired through his loins. Marriage— well, the production of an heir—was something that had loomed in Sebastiano's mind since he'd taken the helm of RBI five years earlier. He wasn't just the person with overall control but its public face. His actions carried as much weight as his words. Choosing the right wife was imperative. It had to be someone respected on her own account, who could act as hostess without being fazed by the company she was keeping, who knew how to moderate her speech and steer away from controversial subjects and knew not to do anything that could bring scandal in its wake, and who was wealthy in her own right. Unfortunately, all the women he knew who fitted these criteria were as exciting as a board meeting. Layla fitted the criteria of the first two aspects. Fear of the damage he would cause would keep her in line for the second two aspects. As she'd already proved herself an opportunistic gold-digger and their marriage would only be brief, the final criterion was moot. That she was a chameleon with fire in her veins would give their brief marriage more entertainment value than all the years of the permanent marriage he would make when it was over.

Openly sweeping his gaze over her bombshell beauty, relishing the defiance in the jut of her chin and the colour slowly creeping over her high cheekbones, he said, 'In public, we will be the model of a respectable couple as befits the head of an international bank.' And then he smiled. 'Whatever war we make between ourselves and whatever form that war takes will be entirely private.'

Layla couldn't settle. Sebastiano had taken himself off to his office and she didn't have it in her to marvel that she was on a private plane with an actual office in it, or marvel at the plush living area she paced up and down in dreaming up myriad scenarios to escape this terrible trap he'd caught her in. Of course, the easiest way out of it was to simply say no and fly back home but this, as with every other scenario, was discarded because they all ended in the same way—her law firm's destruction. Hundreds of current clients with their legal representation ripped away from them. Thousands more future clients lost in the system with nowhere to go for help.

What a fool she'd been. Desperation to get out of her crime-ridden neighbourhood before her baby was born had made her reckless and now she was paying the price. There were only two brief glimmers of sunshine in the whole thing, one being that the money for her baby was already secure—at least for now. She wouldn't put it past Sebastiano to find a way to take it back from her. The other was that during their short marriage, the pregnancy would start to show and Sebastiano would have to confront the truth of it. There was a chance, slim though it was, that her baby might have its father in its life.

His office was at the tail end of the plane. Unable to bear another minute of her own thoughts, she opened the door to it without knocking and found Sebastiano perched on his desk chatting on his phone.

One look at her and he cut the conversation short.

'My beautiful fiancée,' he said, casually placing his phone on the desk without rising from it. 'Missing my company already?'

He'd removed his suit jacket and tie and rolled the sleeves up on his shirt, the muscles of his lean torso clearly delineated beneath the expensive material. Hating herself for what must be an inherent shallowness that her pulses could quicken at the mere sight of him, Layla took a step back to create more distance between them. 'I have questions.'

'And you have come here for the answers? How romantic.'

Gritting her teeth, she prayed to all the gods for strength. 'Did you mean it about donating five million to my law firm?'

'You will learn that I always mean what I say. If the wedding goes smoothly and you put on a convincing act then I will transfer it on Sunday.'

'Why would you do that?'

'Every good dog deserves a bone.'

Her outrage was so immediate that she closed the gap between them in two quick paces and pushed furiously at his chest. 'How can you *say*…?'

A large hand enveloped her wrist, cutting her off mid-outrage. In the blink of a moment, Layla found herself pulled to Sebastiano and trapped between his thighs.

'I probably deserved that reaction, but let's save the kinky stuff for the bedroom,' he murmured.

His position on the desk made them practically eye level. His face was so close to hers that the warmth of his coffee-scented breath landed on her lips. To her absolute horror, warm sensation spread through her veins, and when he speared her hair with the hand not wrapped around her wrist, she was helpless to stop the shiver of delight that zinged down her spine.

'I take back calling you a pig,' she said hoarsely, trying her hardest to wrench her stare from the hypnotic green gaze that was the cause of all this trouble. 'You're nothing but an unmitigated bastard.'

He smiled lazily…lasciviously…and released her

wrist, tiptoeing his fingers up her ribcage and splaying his hand over her right breast to gently pinch the hardened nipple. He pulled her head even closer and, his voice now a seductive whisper, said, 'And what does it say about you that an unmitigated bastard like me turns you into liquid?' And then his sensuous mouth found hers.

CHAPTER FIVE

LAYLA FELL INTO the molten heat of Sebastiano's hungry kiss. For a few heady moments she returned it, winding her arms around his neck and threading her fingers into his hair as their mouths moved together in a ravenous duel of tongues and clashing teeth, her aching breasts—she hadn't even known how badly they'd been aching until he'd touched them—compressed into his hard chest.

For those few heady moments she purged herself, the angst she'd been living with all these months drowning in the feel and taste and scent of the man she'd danced into the fire with...

And who'd burnt her and reduced her to ashes.

Digging her fingernails tightly into his skull, she kissed him even harder, needing him to feel a fraction of the pain his rejection of both her and the life they'd created had caused in her heart, then wrenched her mouth away.

'Do that again and I'll bite your tongue off,' she spat.

Sebastiano tried to think of a retort but his brain was temporarily dead. All his current thinking was coming from a lower part of his anatomy.

It had been like that during their night together, he remembered dimly. A complete capitulation of his body to the sensuous pleasures of Layla. So complete had the capitulation been that his brain—his real one—had fallen too, and when he'd finally been able to drag himself away from her it had been with the sensation that if he couldn't be with her again, his life as he knew it would be over. *He* would be over.

He'd left his suite at the Diamond Club fully intending to be back in her arms by nightfall.

It had been mid-afternoon, sitting with the Governor of the Bank of England, barely able to concentrate on this most important of meetings, that sanity had pushed out the euphoric haze of their lovemaking. Or their sex as his sharpened brain had quickly renamed it.

At the end of the meeting he'd got in the back of his car and ordered his driver to take him to the airport.

The next evening a message from Layla had pinged. He'd read it with his chest so full of an emotion he couldn't discern but which every instinct in his body had recoiled against that he'd come close to throwing his phone in the swimming pool. Instead, he'd made the less extreme choice of blocking her number, then deleted it for good measure too.

He couldn't quite remember his reasoning for this other than the firm conviction that a night of great sex, especially with a bar tender, should not make a man come close to losing his head, but had felt a hell of a lot better in himself for doing it. It was quite possible that he'd sensed her opportunism, he now thought with the great benefit of hindsight. That must have been it. Some unacknowledged sixth sense had warned him Layla would bring trouble on him.

One full-blown kiss and that close-to-drugged feeling had come roaring back. The difference now was that he was going to marry her and have the luxury of revelling in the capitulation. For as long as the marriage lasted he would share a bed with the sexiest woman to walk the earth.

Gazing into her passionately furious forget-me-not eyes, he laughed softly. 'And deny yourself the pleasure you would get from it?'

That wonderful contortion of emotions played over her beautiful face again. And it was wonderful. Glorious. His fiancée was a spitfire of emotion for him.

'If you think *that* is going to happen again, you have another think coming.'

'You think you can resist this chemistry between us?'

'The only chemistry is in your head.'

'Let's see how much it's in my head when you're sharing my bed.'

'That will *never* happen,' she said with such vehemence he almost felt sorry for her.

'You will share my bed for the duration of our marriage or our deal is void.'

Angry colour enflamed her cheeks. 'No way.'

'We have to be convincing, *cara*. I have many staff in my household. I trust their discretion but only to a point—careless words cost lives…or in my case, businesses. I am marrying you to distract the world from my foolish mistake and it has to be convincing or it will backfire. To be convincing you will share my bed.' At her mutinous expression, he smiled and added, 'I will make a deal with you. As my wife you will be obliged to kiss me and show me affection in public, but if I make a move on you in the privacy of our bedroom you reserve the right to bite my tongue off. Fair?'

She managed a nod so tight he could feel the effort it took for her to make it.

'And to prove how reasonable I am and my willingness to show good faith, when you make your move on me, I promise to let you have your way without bloodshed.'

'Never,' she whispered even as her eyes pulsed and her breathing deepened.

Sebastiano inched his face closer to hers and lowered his voice even further to match the volume of hers. 'If you're that revolted by the idea then why are your fingers still in my hair?'

It was the blood pounding in Layla's ears that delayed the horror of what Sebastiano had just pointed out from reaching her hands and enabling her to snatch them away immediately, a delay long enough for the pads of her fingers to continue their slow caress of his skull—when had she stopped digging her nails in to it?—through his soft dark hair.

In an instant she yanked them away and swiped at the hands still buried in her own hair.

Laughing, he put his hands on her waist but before she could react he'd gently steered her back and risen to his feet so she was no longer trapped between his thighs. 'We should take our seats. We'll be landing shortly.'

With the weight of Layla's outraged stare following him, Sebastiano left the office and sauntered back to his seat.

Layla had expected Sebastiano's villa to be big. He was one of the richest men in the world. It was inconceivable that he would live in anything less than grandeur and yet shortly after they'd driven the outskirts of Palermo's colourful streets and into the verdant countryside, the tall trees cleared and there before her was a stunning gold baroque palace that rose from the earth like a pair of angel wings.

'This is yours?' she practically squealed, completely forgetting the vow of silence she'd made in the wake of their kiss. She'd made a pretty good fist of it up to that point though, refusing to exchange a word or glance with him during the landing or the quick march down the plane's steps and into the waiting car. Aggravatingly, her silence and refusal to look at him hadn't perturbed him in the slightest, and she'd had his silky voice and heavy accent polluting her ears by pointing out areas of interest to her during their short drive.

'It is,' he confirmed.

'That's not a villa. It's a palace!'

He chuckled. 'Not quite. It was built in the early eighteenth century for an Italian count but it is very much a villa. It was abandoned for decades. I bought it five years ago. The renovations in the main villa are complete but a number of the guest cottages are still to be finished.'

The long drive was flanked by a sprawling landscaped lawn so thickly green and vast it reminded her of the gardens of the English palaces and castles she'd visited with her mother over the years. The closer they drove to it, the more the villa's beauty revealed itself. Soon she saw the gold was an illusion caused by the sun, the walls painted a pristine white, the tall sash windows and frames and roof a gleaming sandstone colour.

'How many bedrooms does it have?'

'Fourteen in the main villa but the guest cottages and lodges can sleep another thirty people. The staff have their own quarters.'

It made her feel quite faint. 'All this for one man?'

'One day it will be a family home filled with children.'

It should not feel like another twist of the knife to know the family he was envisaging did not include her own baby.

Determined to hide it, she airily said, 'Can I bagsy a room for our child, then?'

'If by bagsy you mean choose then of course. Choose whichever room you wish for your imaginary baby.'

'Go and buy a pregnancy test for me to take,' she said on impulse. 'You will see with your own eyes that I *am* pregnant.'

He laughed. 'You are tenacious, I will give you that. And if it does show that you are pregnant, what then? You cannot expect me to believe the child is mine.'

She could have screamed her frustration. 'You are incredible.'

'Thank you.'

'It wasn't a compliment.'

'I know.'

'I've already got the money. Why would I still need to lie?' she demanded.

'Because to admit the truth would mean admitting to the lie, and, before you start shouting at me again, we are about to go inside and be amongst staff so I need you to practise your *complete adoration* face.'

'You are going to be a father! We have created a life together! How can you expect me to walk around the home you're intending to fill with babies from another woman looking all pathetic and adoring when you're stubbornly refusing to accept that you already have a child on the way with *me*?'

A sudden warning flashed from his green eyes, all sardonic amusement vanishing. 'Do not test me, Layla. There are members of my staff I would trust with my life but we both know everyone has their price. I do not want to destroy a charitable law firm that does such good, so do not put me in a position where I have to destroy yours.'

Clenching her fists, she let out her frustration with a long, gritted-teeth scream and a stamp of her feet, then blew out a long breath of air, shook her hands loose, straightened her back and smiled. 'Lead the way, *darling*. I'm just *so* excited to finally be at the home we're going to lead a long and happy life together in.'

His eyes narrowed before a glimmer of amusement flashed back in them. 'That hurt, didn't it?'

Not dropping her smile, she nodded brightly. 'So very much.'

'Poor Layla.' He tapped on his door. It opened immediately.

Once he was out, Layla accepted his offered hand with a, 'Thank you, *darling*.'

He brought her hand to his mouth and razed his lips over her knuckles. *'Il piacere e tutto mio.'*

She gazed at him with open adoration. 'I've no idea what you just said but I'm sure it was wonderfully romantic.'

'Wonderfully,' he agreed. 'I can teach you my language, if you like?'

'I would be *thrilled*,' she cooed putting her hand to her heart.

He burst into laughter, palmed her cheek and murmured, 'Possibly turn it down a notch?'

She covered his hand and gazed into his eyes with a dreamy sigh. 'Too much?'

Amusement still writ on his face, he threaded his fingers through hers and led her through the magnificent arched entrance flanked by marble statues of men—Layla assumed Roman gods—in toga-style robes reading books.

The mid-afternoon Sicilian sun was far hotter than the sun they'd left behind in London and she welcomed the cool interior of the reception room, welcomed even more the fresh orange juice served by a smartly dressed middle-aged man with the shiniest shoes she'd ever seen as it gave her a legitimate reason to unthread her fingers from Sebastiano's.

Clutching tightly to her glass, she walked beside him through palatially sized rooms with high frescoed ceilings, the dominant colour gold, and tried to ignore the awareness zinging through her veins at his closeness by concentrating all her attention on the ornate interiors that would feel at home in any palace.

'This is nothing like I expected,' she commented as she was shown into a dining room so vast it could accommodate her entire workforce and clientele.

'What did you expect?' he asked.

She shrugged. 'Something much more modern. This feels like I've stepped back in time, and when I compare it to your suite at the Diamond Club...'

'Everything here has been renovated sympathetically. You do not buy a villa built for royalty and turn it into a play den.'

'The Diamond Club's building must be as old as this and you turned your suite there into a play den,' she pointed out.

'That's because I use it as a play den. It's a place for me to switch off and entertain my real friends, whereas this place… Just as I am the public face of my bank, this is the public face of me. It is a villa that befits my status and projects wealth, taste, capability and a serious mindset.'

She snorted.

He caught her eye and gave a wry smile. 'I run a multi-billion-euro bank, *cara*. I entertain world leaders within these walls.'

'So no table football here?'

'Image is everything in my world. Let me show you the ballroom where we'll be hosting our wedding reception and then you can freshen up before we eat.'

'I've nothing to freshen up with,' she reminded him.

'Have you not yet noticed that I think of everything?'

'Apart from effective contraception,' she riposted so sweetly that the curdling poison that infected Sebastiano's blood every time she mentioned the pregnancy was muted by the amusement threading like waves through his veins.

Layla's luminescent beauty was the first thing he'd noticed about her, the years revealing a subtle wit that came only in infrequent flashes and only ever when they were alone and she was pouring him drinks as he relaxed from the stress of his job. All those hours spent together, revealing much of himself—it was only when he looked back on those hours that he realised how much he'd given away to her—but without her revealing anything of herself. He'd never asked. Never wanted to know. Layla had been his secret pleasure, a beautiful, sexy sounding board who listened attentively without venturing her own opinions. It was her lack of opinions that had led him to believe she listened without understanding. Let him believe there was little going on in her head.

He'd made the fatal error of underestimating her. He'd forgotten that she'd been paid to serve him. Paid to blend into the background unless called to the forefront. Paid to cater to his needs and be whoever he needed her to be.

It was with not a little discomfort that he acknowledged that he'd needed her to be a decorative adornment and had revelled in her adopting that role for him. Had revelled in the sexual charge that had grown between them during their hours together. Had arrogantly assumed she'd resigned her job at the club so that unspoken sexual charge could be acted on.

Their night together had blown his mind. He'd known they'd be good together but couldn't have guessed just how good it would be. Not just the sex but the laughter that had come with it. Sex with Layla had been hot and fun and all-consuming.

It was only now with all their gloves off that he was seeing the real Layla emerge, a feisty, quick-witted beauty with hands that spoke their own language and facial expressions and eyes that told you exactly what she was thinking. He could only imagine the restraint it must have taken for her not to let her mask slip when working at the club.

'I am a man of immense wealth, *cara*,' he told her, matching the faux sweetness of her smile, 'and I can assure you I purchase only the best in contraception.' And there had been nothing during their night together to suggest it had failed for them. Nothing at all. Sure, there were a few shadows in their night together where the all-consuming nature of their coupling came to him as sensory imprints rather than concrete memories, but at no point had he failed to wear a condom.

And yet...

He blinked away the flicker of doubt that suddenly tugged at him as ruthlessly as he'd blinked it away the other times it had tugged at him.

'And I can assure you,' she said, not dropping the sweet act, 'that you need to ask for a refund.'

Layla followed Sebastiano up a wide sweeping marble staircase that belonged in a fairy tale and found herself so overwhelmed as more of the villa's majestic beauty opened itself up to her that she only listened with half an ear to him say, 'A design team is on its way. They will bring a selection of clothing to go through with you so they can learn your style, and source and create a suitable new wardrobe for you.'

'Suitable?' She craned her neck to fully take in the spectacular mezzanine the stairs led onto.

'Suitable for the wife of Sebastiano Russo.'

'Referring to yourself in the third person? Classy.'

'It often feels that the public Sebastiano Russo is his own singular persona.'

'And you expect me to create a matching persona as your wife?'

'It will be easy for you. You have already proven yourself a consummate actress. The design team will be here within the hour—I've had a room put aside for you to work with them. Once the wedding is announced, they will work with you to create a dress to marry in.' He turned his stare to her and, with a tone of the utmost regret, said, 'I know it will pain you to hear this, but we will both be kept busy before the wedding and so you will see little of me until the big day itself.'

As they were passing a room with the door open and two members of uniformed staff making up a four-poster bed, Layla made sure to look suitably crestfallen. 'Oh, that is devastating.'

His regretful expression lifted. The gleam she so loathed and yet which made her pulses soar returned to his eyes. 'Be assured you will have the pleasure of my company every night in our bed.'

Sniffing an opportunity, she put her hands to her racing heart and fluttered her eyelashes. 'Oh, darling, I wouldn't want to scandalise the staff by sharing a bed out of wedlock, so why don't I sleep in a guest room until our big day?'

They'd reached the end of the mezzanine. Leaning against a marble pillar, he caressed her cheek. 'You are so thoughtful but the staff have already prepared my room for your arrival.'

She affectionately covered the hand resting against her cheek and dug her nails in. 'Then I shall make sure to get the design team to source some all-in-one pyjamas for me.'

He tutted and murmured, 'Image, *cara*, image. What will the staff think if you wear pyjamas in bed? You will find a selection of lingerie and nightwear already unpacked in your dressing room. Come, I will show you.'

With that, he opened the door to an intensely masculine room of deep green with goldleaf etchings patterned on the walls and ceiling, and heavy deep green drapes. The furniture was all dark wood, the soft furnishings a muted olive, the bedspread of the ginormous four-poster with tied-back dark green curtains black. If the room weren't so vast in size and if light weren't pouring in through the three sash windows running from floor to ceiling, she would think it oppressive. Instead, her first impression was that it was seductive. Her first instinct was to back right away and stay behind the threshold.

He stood behind her. 'You like?'

She was having trouble taking her eyes off the bed. All she could picture was Sebastiano lying on it naked, a lascivious gleam in his eyes as he beckoned her to him...

Heated pulses fluttered low in her pelvis. Very much aware of the cleaning staff so close by, she had to swallow to huskily say, 'Bit dark for my tastes but it certainly suits you.'

However aware she was of the cleaning staff, it had nothing on her awareness for Sebastiano. Seeing the bed she would sleep beside him in for nights with no defined end to them...

Hands gently gripped her biceps. A hard, lean body pressed into her back. Hot breath swirled in her hair, then a deep inhalation as if he were breathing her in before his lips touched the rim of her ear and, his fingers

kneading into her skin, knuckles brushing the sides of
her breasts, he whispered, 'Tell me you're not already
imagining sharing the bed with me.'

CHAPTER SIX

LAYLA WAS THRILLINGLY aware of his hardness pressing into her lower back, the fluttering pulses in her pelvis becoming molten liquid. Close to swaying, she felt her breasts tingle wildly in anticipation of Sebastiano's hands sliding from her arms to cover them, the compulsion to lean her head back onto his shoulder and into the crook of his neck...

It took a major burst of impetus to pull herself away and step into the safety of the bedroom.

Striding to a window, she fixed her gaze over the rear of the villa and what was possibly the most stunning vista she'd ever seen, and snatched as much air as she could into lungs that had lost the ability to breathe. 'Shut the door.'

The breathlessness of Layla's order tightened Sebastiano's arousal to a point.

Dio, it felt like he'd been aroused from the moment he'd opened his eyes. The knowledge he would end his day with Layla Sansom lying beside him had crowded his mind before the dreams of sleep had cleared.

And now she was here. The opportunistic hustler was going to pay her debt to him by distracting the world from the foolishness of his actions—or, to be technical, his inactions—with a marriage that would be short but in no way sweet.

She couldn't know it but she'd already repaid some of her debt. Bringing her here, all the planning that had gone into it, all the anticipation of it, had all served as the distraction he'd needed to the potential destruction of his reputation and the potential destruction of the business that had belonged to his family for half a millennia. It had stopped him thinking about it in any depth at all.

She spun around before he reached her. 'You said the bedroom would be a safe space from your wandering hands so back off.'

He held his hands up and murmured, 'I didn't put it in quite those words.'

'The intention was the same, so keep your distance.'

'What are you afraid of, *cara*? That you won't be able to restrain yourself?' The fire that blazed in those fabulous forget-me-not eyes at this... 'Has anyone told you that you're beautiful when you're angry?'

'Has anyone told you that you need to come up with some new lines because that one's so old it's beyond stale?'

'As enjoyable as it is to feel your passion for me—'

'My *what*?'

'Your passion, currently displaying itself as anger—I need you to put it on ice. Time is moving. Your design team will arrive soon and you will display all the signs of a woman excited about her new life with the love of her life. Is that clear?'

The Medusa effect of her stare didn't diminish an inch. 'You have already made that clear. Outside the walls of this bedroom, complete adoration.' She folded her arms over her breasts and spun back around to gaze out of the window.

There was something in Layla's rigid, stubborn stance, a hint of vulnerability that, just for a moment, made Sebastiano's heart catch and throat close.

It took a longer moment to shake the unsettling reactions off.

'Who do you want to invite to the wedding?' he asked, standing beside her at the window.

Thrown at the change of subject, Layla couldn't stop herself turning her stare back to him.

'We have four full days to make the arrangements. It will look odd if you don't have anyone from your side,' he reasoned.

'We can't have that,' she muttered, knowing he was right but in no mood to let go of her anger even though Sebastiano had already called it out for what it was.

How could one man make a woman *feel* so much?

She needed to get a grip on herself and her emotions quickly because this was only the beginning.

Fixing her gaze on the deep blue sea just beyond the thick trees that served as the perimeter to his estate, she took a deep breath. 'What do we tell people about how we came to be together?'

'Exactly what I told Laurence—the truth. I met you at the Diamond Club, we were secret lovers and only once you left did I realise I had fallen in love with you.'

Well, that made her heart wrench. 'I thought you just said we'd be telling the truth.'

'Sticking to the truth as much as we can so we don't get caught out in a lie.'

'I can't lie to my mum.' She looked again at him. 'She already knows about you.'

His eyebrows drew together. 'What does she know?'

'That you're the father of my baby. That you ghosted and blocked me.' She shrugged with deliberate nonchalance.

She would never tell him of her utter desolation when she'd realised that he'd blocked her number, when her numerous calls to him had failed to connect and her desperate text message of, *I'm pregnant and frightened, please call me*, didn't even make it to delivered status. She'd found her mum curled up on the sofa watching one of her soap operas, crocheting. Her mum had looked up at her and simply said, 'Are you ready to tell me what's going on with you?'

And so she had.

'Does she know about the money you blackmailed from me?'

'Yes. I can't lie to her, Seb.'

She knew from the movement in his green eyes that he was thinking hard. 'Can she be trusted?'

'Yes, so you don't need to make any more threats—I will play my part and she will play hers. I know what's at stake if we don't make this convincing. She won't breathe a word to anyone.'

His eyes continued to bore into hers.

'You can trust her,' she reiterated into the silence.

He gave a sharp nod and looked at his watch. 'Then I shall take you at your word. Now come, let me show you your dressing room and where everything is. I have much to do.'

* * *

With Layla firmly ensconced in his home and the design team creating a wardrobe that befitted her as his wife, Sebastiano focused his attention on everything else. The press release was ready to go, all the preparations for the wedding were discreetly underway, the members of his core team working on damage limitation were readying to firefight if necessary, senior members of the bank prepared for a potentially damaging news story and spoonfed the official line to take…everything was in hand. Everything had been considered from every angle. Everyone knew the part they had to play.

As far as his family, his directors and core team were concerned, he was sticking with the truth as he'd explained it to Layla. He would not have any of them think he'd had to threaten her and her law firm with destruction to obtain her agreement. If it turned out she really was pregnant…

Well, that would serve a purpose of its own, but he would not think about that, not with the tugging doubt in his stomach growing stronger now she was finally here with him.

It was being with her. Watching her graceful movements. Gazing into forget-me-not eyes that ranged in expression from naked desire to open loathing and fury, often within a blink.

The expression on her face when the household butler escorted her into the smaller dining room was the complete adoration he demanded of her.

He rose to greet her.

His chameleon had changed, the sexy but plain tight trousers and top replaced by a colourful halter-neck dress that fell to mid-thigh and showcased the fabulous legs he'd admired for so long. Her long hair had been scooped into a loose bun, tendrils framing her face, large, hooped gold earrings and a thick Egyptian-style bracelet adorning her skin, and he felt a stab of satisfaction that the vast range of jewellery he'd had couriered over for her use contained items that suited her so well.

She closed in on him, enveloping his senses in a cloud of sultry perfume. He'd had thirty scents brought in for her, figuring she would like at least one of them. The one she'd chosen made him hungry to breathe it directly off her skin.

It wasn't until she put a hand to his shoulder that he saw the challenge in her eyes. 'Good evening, darling,' she said breathily, before rising onto her toes and kissing him. Not a brief greeting of a kiss, but a deep, sensuous locking of mouths that caught him unprepared. When she broke it, she pouted another kiss, winked, and then slid into the chair set beside his that the butler had pulled out for her. The serenity in both her stance and her actions would have made him laugh if he weren't fighting to stop his arousal from showing.

'I think I prefer this dining room to the one you showed me earlier,' she commented brightly. 'Much more intimate.'

He cleared his throat and retook his seat. 'This one is for personal use. The other is for entertaining.'

A member of staff leaned between them to pour her wine but she covered the glass with her hand. 'Just water for me, please.'

Their food was served and then Sebastiano dismissed the staff so it was just the two of them.

Damn but he was still aroused.

Taking a drink of his wine, he passed a large envelope to her. 'Our prenuptial agreement,' he told her.

She sighed dreamily as she took it from him. 'You have romance in your soul.'

'I'm Sicilian. Romance is in my blood.'

The dreamy expression didn't drop. 'And there was me thinking it was vengeance you bled.'

'We are a people of passion in all its forms.' Just as Layla was a woman of passion, a thought that didn't help with the throbbing between his legs. He handed her a pen. 'There will be no negotiating any of the contents. All I require is your signature.'

'I'm sure the agreement is a testament to your generosity,' she riposted, peeling the envelope open and removing the document. 'However, I would be a terrible lawyer to put my signature to a document I didn't read first, plus I'm keen to learn how much of my vast fortune I need to pay you when we go our separate ways.'

Her witty irreverence made him laugh, and as he watched her read it while they dined on *pollo ai funchi*, he wondered again what it had taken to hide this side of herself when she'd worked at the club.

As she read, her serenity slowly leeched out until she put her cutlery down to look at him. 'I can't sign this. It's—'

'It is not open to negotiation,' he cut in.

'It says that if our marriage ends within a year then you'll pay me fifty million euros. Sebastiano, you're forcing me to marry you as a punishment, so why would you—?'

'I cannot be seen to give you anything less than I would in a real marriage.'

Her shoulders made a slight slump before she lifted her chin again. 'The clauses about children...'

'Again, nothing less than would be expected in a real marriage and again, nothing that is open to negotiation—none of it is. Sign it or the deal is off.'

Her eyes held his, something thoughtful flickering in the forget-me-nots before she picked up the pen and signed.

He nodded his approval and dabbed the sides of his mouth with a napkin. 'Who knew blackmail would prove so lucrative? Now you will have to excuse me—I have a video conference with Zurich. I will see you later in bed.'

Until Layla's night with Sebastiano, she'd been the soundest of sleepers. Since that night though, sleep had been erratic, morphing into full-blown insomnia after she'd blackmailed the money from him. The last thing she'd expected as she rummaged in her dressing room for something to sleep in that wouldn't make the staff suspicious and which wouldn't send 'come and get me' signals to Sebastiano was to fall asleep within moments of her head hitting the pillow.

So soundly did she sleep that when she opened her eyes she was disoriented to find the room filled with dusky light and Sebastiano standing on the other side of the bed scrolling through his phone, dressed in smart navy trousers and a pale blue shirt, different clothing than what he'd worn for dinner.

Her heart ballooned and caught in her throat.

He noticed her looking and a wry smile spread across his handsome face. 'Ah, the Sleeping Beauty awakens.'

'It's morning?' she whispered.

'Eight o'clock.'

She could hardly believe it. When she'd checked her phone after the long video call with her mother in which she'd filled her in on everything and in which her mother had been love and understanding itself, it had been ten-thirty p.m. She'd snuggled under the covers straight after saying goodnight to her.

She was almost frightened to see if the other side of the bed had been slept in.

'I assumed you'd be waiting for me with a taser in your hand when I came up but you were dead to the world,' he said, as if he'd read her mind. 'Did you know you talk in your sleep?'

If her hands weren't holding the bedsheets so tightly, she'd have clutched her burning cheeks.

'It was mostly mumbles,' he said with a wink before strolling over and perching his backside on the bed close to her.

Immediately her senses were assailed by the scent of freshly clean Sebastiano and, as their eyes clashed, for one wild moment she was overtaken by a longing for him to rip the bedsheets off her.

She tightened her grip on the sheets and cocooned herself deeper into them.

The smile that played on his lips told her he knew exactly what she was thinking, and when he opened his mouth, she braced herself, certain he would say something sexy and suggestive.

'I need you to get up and dressed.'

Well, that threw her. Sebastiano was telling her to put clothes on when she'd been anticipating him suggesting she remove what little she was wearing.

'Today is going to be a roller coaster, for all of us,' he reminded her. Reminding her of the reason he'd chosen the marriage route as his vengeance. Revenge and reputation management in one fell swoop. Not for the little life they'd created together.

'Has the article about you gone live yet?'

He shook his head. 'I have it on good authority that it will be posted before eleven. We will give it ten minutes for people to notice and share it, and then we release the news of our engagement.'

'Why wait those ten minutes?'

'So the journalist isn't tempted to retract and release it at a later date. We're burying bad news, not delaying it, so get yourself ready and, while we wait, prepare the list of guests you wish to invite with contact details for them. Your new assistant will make the arrangements to bring them here while you work with the design team on your wedding dress.'

'You've employed an assistant for me?'

'You will find it necessary. As my wife your diary will overflow with invitations which need to be managed with our individual work commitments. Your assistant will work in tandem with mine.' His phone pinged in his hand. He got up from the bed, reading it. 'My team's arrived. When you're ready, come and join us.'

The moment Sebastiano disappeared through the bedroom door, the tight control Layla had been clinging to released in a rush. Her heart and lungs exploded, blood zooming to the roots of her hair and the tips of her toes.

Hot tears prickled her eyes and she frantically blinked them away, swallowing hard while breathing equally hard through her nose. Her physical responses to Sebastiano were completely beyond her control, she already knew that. But waking from a deep sleep in the intimacy of his bedroom and him being the first thing she saw... His scent the first thing she inhaled...

It was a long while before she felt enough in control of her limbs to safely climb off the bed and pad across the room to her bathroom that adjoined her dressing room, which itself adjoined Sebastiano's dressing room, which in turn adjoined his own bathroom. No his-and-hers sinks in the master bedroom of Sebastiano's villa. Here there were his-and-hers bathrooms, and hers was the prettiest she'd ever had the pleasure of using, a retreat with a strong Japanese influence that she could lock herself away from the world in.

Lock herself away from Sebastiano and the sexual magnetism she responded so viscerally to.

She still felt shaky under the powerful spray of the shower, and as she lathered silky shampoo into her hair, her thoughts drifted to the clauses in the prenuptial agreement. What had been behind them? She hadn't misread them. They'd been translated into English as masterfully as Sebastiano spoke it.

Had they come from him or his legal team?

Custody of any child born within the marriage will be shared on an equal basis...

It was the *born within the marriage* part she couldn't wrap her head around. Why wouldn't he make the clause state any child *conceived* within the marriage? She'd sensed him doubting his own stance on the pregnancy but sensed too an entrenchment in the belief that if she was pregnant, the child could not be his. So why add that clause? Why make provisions for a child you didn't believe to be your own?

Was it a case of hedging his bets? Saving face? Or something else, something deeper?

She was still pondering it all as she went through the clothes she'd selected from the racks of clothing the design team had brought for her to choose from the day before and which had fitted her perfectly. Her mind still firmly on Sebastiano, she selected a pair of white three-quarter-length slim-fitting jeans and an elegant white silk blouse embroidered with red orchids. Dressed, pastries eaten and orange juice drunk, she was about to set off and find the man she was only four days away from marrying when she felt something she could only describe as a flutter in her belly.

Stilling, she didn't even dare to breathe, not until she felt it a second time and, with excitement coursing through her veins, she scrambled to undo her jeans and palm the still-flat surface of her belly.

The fluttering had stopped but...did her stomach feel thicker beneath her hand?

She turned on her side in front of the full-length mirror, lifted her blouse, and then slumped in dejection. Not even the semblance of a bump.

It didn't matter, she told herself, lifting her shoulders back up. She'd experienced the first real physical sign of the pregnancy since an order of barbecued ribs had made her nauseous a few weeks back.

She'd felt her baby.

Her and Sebastiano's baby.

* * *

Sebastiano sat at the desk of his home office surrounded by his core team. Everyone had crammed themselves onto the various forms of hard and soft seating, all scrolling through phones and refreshing laptops. Instead of following suit, he found his attention kept being drawn to the open door of the adjoining office, appointed to his soon-to-be wife. Layla was in there, going through her guest list and other aspects of the wedding and her working life with her new assistant.

Since she'd strolled into his office with a bright, 'This must be the war room,' before giving him a kiss that was just the right side of passionate in a working environment, the frayed edges of his nerves had soothed somewhat. Introducing her to his team and her new assistant, showing her to her office, had all helped distract from the gnawing knowledge that this could be the day he destroyed one of the world's oldest banks. And because he couldn't let that happen, he would have no choice but to resign his position. His reputation would be dust. There was no one in the Russo family lined up to take over. No one suitable. His parents had both retired from the board and as they'd been the ones to groom him into the role, they would be tainted by association. Sebastiano was an only child. With the exception of Paolo, his Russo cousins had all forged diverging careers. Sebastiano enjoyed Paolo's company immensely, trusted him to run the European branch, but that was with Sebastiano's hawk-eyed oversight. If Paolo weren't a Russo, he wouldn't have made it past customer complaints.

If Sebastiano fell, Russo Banca Internazionale would

be forced to appoint a non-Russo to lead it for the first time in its long, distinguished history.

'It's live,' someone suddenly said into the silence. 'Linking it now.'

Sebastiano held his breath as he waited for the link to ping.

He'd hardly read the main headline when he felt a pair of eyes on him. Looking up from the screen, he saw Layla standing in the doorway, taking it all in.

Their eyes met.

After the longest time passed her chest rose and her neck extended, and then as she exhaled she gave a smile so soft his thumping heart flipped over.

A burst of fire zinged through his veins. Filling his lungs, Sebastiano slammed his palm on the table and said, 'Five more minutes and then we bury this.'

For the second night in a row, Layla was fast asleep before Sebastiano came to bed. This time though, she'd lain awake for an age, palming her belly, hoping with all her heart for another fluttering. Her brain had been too wired to simply switch straight off.

Sebastiano's plan seemed to be working exactly as envisaged. Once the press release about their marriage had gone out, the phones of all the people in his war room had gone berserk. Nine out of ten of the calls had been about the wedding, only ten per cent about the billion-euro loss. Social media was ablaze, digital newspapers all leading with the wedding. Layla's phone had come close to conking out in protest at the hundreds of messages received, many from people she'd had no contact with since secondary school.

While Sebastiano and his team dealt with the media scrum, Layla had been kept busy with the wedding. Everything was already in hand but, to her surprise, she was given the final choice on canapés and the courses that would be served for their wedding banquet, and asked to approve the final colour scheme. It hadn't occurred to her that her input would be wanted. She had imagined all that would be required of her was to turn up at the appointed time and look suitably adoring.

There had been no time to wonder why this should be though, as Sebastiano had brought her a top-of-the-range laptop and liaised with Laurence about connecting it to Clayton Community Law's intranet.

She found it strangely touching that he understood how important her work was. Whether it was for show or not—he'd preordained that their respective workaholic tendencies would destroy their marriage—he'd gone out of his way to ensure she had everything needed to make working in the villa comfortable and efficient until her designated date of return to the office. As that designated date was four weeks away, Layla had spent the rest of the day liaising with colleagues—all of whom bombarded her with questions about Sebastiano—about how to manage her clients in the interim, also squeezing in the time to offer the full asking price for the suburban house. The offer was accepted in minutes. When her fake marriage to Sebastiano was over, she could move straight into it. In the meantime she would continue working on her mother to move into it from the second it was legally hers.

By the time she'd finished eating dinner with Sebastiano and his team, who'd continued discussing and strategising throughout the meal, her eyes had been gritty with exhaustion.

It had been Sebastiano who'd looked at her wan face and gently suggested she get some sleep.

Whether that gentleness was for show or not, she didn't know, but she'd lain in his huge bed for an age before drifting off, his face firmly in her mind, holding her belly in the hope of feeling his baby move again, all with the lingering taste of his light goodnight kiss on her mouth and a lingering tingle on the exact spot his stubbly cheek had brushed hers.

CHAPTER SEVEN

SEBASTIANO WAS USED to working long hours, but this was something else. Everything was proceeding as planned but pockets of fire kept flaring that all needed to be doused, and that was on top of the workload that came with running an international bank along with ensuring he was on top of his workload enough to take a week off as a sop to a honeymoon, and came with organising the wedding of the century at incredibly short notice.

He'd had the earth's sexiest creature under his roof and in his bed for three days and been too busy to spend more than snatches of time alone with her.

His current workload had him working each night until the early hours. He would climb the stairs to his room, the entirety of his being inflating to know Layla was already in there. He'd slip beneath the covers beside her sleeping form torn between making noise and movement enough to wake her and not wanting to disturb the peace of her sleep. It had to be all that fiery passion burning her energy through the day that allowed her to sleep for the dead.

Although their time alone together had come in snatches, their shared meals and adjoining offices meant he'd had much opportunity to observe her, and when he reached the dividing threshold and found her on a telephone call, he instinctively knew from the tone of her voice that she was talking to one of her clients. On the desk that formed an L with hers, Giovanna, Layla's assistant, looked up from her computer, gave a nervous smile of greeting before immediately looking back at her screen.

Layla took much longer to meet his eye, but when she did, a smile curved her cheeks and something glimmered in her eyes he was quite certain she was unaware of.

She held up a finger to indicate she'd be one minute.

Waiting was no bother, not when it meant he got a whole minute of observing his fiancée unhindered.

How was it possible for someone's beauty to grow by the day?

How was it possible for desire to turn on with the ease of a tap just to catch a glimpse of someone or catch a waft of their perfume?

Today she was wearing a dark blue maxi-dress, the buttons running its length opened to show the merest hint of cleavage, her hair in her favoured loose style. Having observed her so much, he now understood why she preferred it loose: she was always fiddling with it, whether running her fingers through it, tucking strands behind her ears or winding strands around her fingers. He could still feel the sensation of those fingers scraping through his own hair...

She ended her call and smiled at him. 'Did you need me for something?'

He had the perfect answer for that but, with Giovanna working so close to them and no doubt hearing every word exchanged, he settled for sitting on the edge of

Layla's desk. Having an audience, though, gave him a legitimate excuse to lean over and stroke her cheek. 'I had a few minutes free and thought I would check in with my beautiful fiancée before she's whisked away for her dress fitting.'

The colour that enflamed her cheeks at his touch was an aphrodisiac all of its own.

The design team had moved into the villa so they could work around the clock on her wedding dress and that afternoon had been set aside for Layla's first proper fitting. Whatever direction the design of the dress took, she would be the most beautiful bride to have ever graced Sicilian soil. He traced the rim of her ear, delighting in her almost imperceptible shiver.

From the moment Sebastiano slipped into her office, Layla had been wholly aware of his presence and now, her cheek and ear aflame from his touch, she was having to fight to stop the entirety of her senses becoming consumed by him. Clearing her throat, she said in a voice she needed no effort to make sound husky, 'I'm not wanted for another half-hour.'

He pressed his cheek against hers and whispered, 'Believe me, *cara*, you are *always* wanted.'

She could do nothing to stop her breath hitching and when he pulled back and she caught the gleam in his beautiful green eyes, she knew he'd heard it, and when he reached again to stroke her cheek, the thumps of her heart were so strong she was certain he must be able to hear them too.

His desirous stare not leaving hers, he said, 'Giovanna, can you give us two minutes please?'

Layla's assistant left the office and closed the door without a murmur.

Alone with Sebastiano, her heart thumping erratically, Layla tried to wrench her stare from his, tried even harder to fight the thrills of anticipation lacing her blood at the mouth closing in on hers...

The tip of his nose brushed against her. His breath was hot on her face...

'In case I forget to mention it later, my parents and grandparents and a few other relatives will be joining us for dinner this evening,' he murmured. 'Formal dress. I will go through behavioural expectations later.'

Layla's butterfly-laden stomach turned over and she reared back.

A knowing smile played on his lips. The bastard knew exactly the effect he had on her and was positively revelling in it.

'Don't look so alarmed. They won't eat you,' he teased. 'They might *want* to eat you...' His eyes glimmered. Her pelvis clenched. 'Not in the same way as *I* want to eat you, of course, but my family are old-school courteous and they wouldn't dream of being rude to you. Not to your face.'

She had to scramble through the fog of blood roaring in her head to drag out, 'What have you told them about me?'

'What I have told everyone else.' The firm lips her mouth was tingling with need to feel compressed upon it were barely a feather away from making contact. 'That you are my lover and that there is nothing I wouldn't do to make you mine.'

Layla didn't know if it was a sob of relief or disappointment that hitched up her throat when he pulled away from her and returned to his own office.

Sebastiano had known his chameleon fiancée would charm his extremely proper, socially conscious family, and so it proved from the moment she swished into the dining room wrapped in a slinky black cocktail dress with her hair piled in a loose bun, loose tendrils and large hooped earrings framing her perfect face. Being seated opposite her meant that, though he had to forgo the pleasure of feeling the heat of her body beside him and inhaling the sultry scent of her perfume, he had the pleasure of watching her. And it was a pleasure. Not a single expression on her beautiful face or movement of her body was anything less than mesmerising. Whenever their eyes locked, he caught a shimmer in hers, a remnant of the desire that had blazed earlier and which sent a shimmer of it straight back into his loins.

Only the knowledge that the villa was overrun with hundreds of staff and external workers busy transforming it for the wedding had stopped him pressing his mouth to hers for the kiss her lips had parted for.

Layla wanted him. He knew it. And she knew he knew it.

Throughout their five-course meal, she played the part he'd given her to perfection, proving herself as graceful and elegant and learned as they could wish for a new family member, especially one who would be so prominent. His mother studied her the closest but his grandfather was smitten before the main course had been served. As for Paolo, Sebastiano's cousin and best man for the wedding, he found himself on the receiving end of death stares from his wife for his failure to remove his eyes from Layla's face, death stares he was completely oblivious to.

'Don't you drink, Layla?' Sebastiano's father asked when she poured herself another glass of iced water.

Her mesmerising forget-me-not eyes darted to Sebastiano before she bestowed his father with the lopsided smile that could break a man's heart at fifty paces. 'Not when I need to keep a clear head for my wedding,' she quipped, which made his father laugh and his mother's eyes narrow.

Sebastiano thought back to all the meals they'd shared these last few days. She'd stuck to water in all of them. Not a drop of alcohol had passed her lips since her arrival here.

She did drink though. They'd shared a bottle of champagne the night they'd spent together.

A pulse throbbed in his temple.

Why keep up the act of being pregnant when there was nothing to be gained? Layla was smart enough to know he couldn't pull out of the wedding now. She was legally minded enough to know the prenuptial agreement was watertight and the fifty million would be hers from the moment they signed the certificate. Those of the world's press who hadn't already set up camp at the villa's gates were scurrying as fast as they could to join them. It was too late to cancel—

He suddenly noticed she had a hand resting lightly on her belly. Noticed, too, the gentle strokes of her fingers. The animation on her face as she continued charming his father suggested she wasn't even aware she was doing it.

The pulse turned into a pounding. The surrounding

conversations had become distant white noise. Closing his eyes in a long blink in an effort to clear it, Sebastiano opened them to find Layla's beautiful eyes dart back on him.

His heart made a heavy thump against his ribs.

Their gazes held.

The white noise vanished into nothing.

The strangest sensation loosened in the centre of his chest. He was barely aware of it spreading to cover his lungs, not until it had squeezed the breath from them.

Layla tugged her hand out of Sebastiano's and, without saying a word, headed straight to her bathroom.

Closing the door, she rested a hand to her pounding heart. She was struggling to breathe. For the first time since her arrival in Sicily, Sebastiano had come to bed with her.

She removed her makeup and brushed her teeth with shaking hands.

It had taken every sinew of effort to put her focus on playing the role Sebastiano demanded of her for his family. Every sinew because all her eyes had wanted to do was stare at him. Every sinew because the ache that had opened in anticipation of the kiss that had never come still burned. Just to be held in his gaze intensified it.

And now they were alone. No audience to play for. Nothing to distract her from the pulses beating in her throat and the heat between her legs.

Nothing at all to distract her from *him*.

How on earth was she going to manage their 'honeymoon' week, she wondered helplessly when she padded into her dressing room. Come Sunday morning and Sebastiano's helicopter would fly them to the tiny Mediterranean island bought by the Russo family as the perfect romantic, private getaway. With only a skeleton staff there, it would essentially be just the two of them. No work or other distractions. For a whole week.

A 'honeymoon wardrobe' had already been prepared for her by her design team. She didn't dare ask what it consisted of or hope it involved more than string bikinis and sexy lingerie.

The lingerie couldn't be worse than what she already had. The worst of it was how much her skin sang to wear it. Beautiful matching underwear for the day, delicate silk camis for the night. She had to rummage through the latter to find one that actually covered her buttocks, settling on a cream silk number that still left little to the imagination.

She felt almost sick with nerves but it was a different kind of sickness from the occasional mild nausea she'd experienced in the first few months of the pregnancy. This was a sickness of anticipation.

Desperate to have better control of herself before she joined him in the bedroom, Layla slipped her arms into a kimono-style robe and then called her mum. Just to hear her voice and know she would be joining her here in the morning, an ally in an overwhelming world, soothed a little of Layla's frayed edges.

But only a little. Once the call was finished, she was out of distractions.

She could put it off no more. She was going to have to get into bed with Sebastiano for the first time since they'd conceived their child.

Taking a deep breath, she tightened the robe and opened the dressing room door.

Sebastiano was in bed reading something on his phone. His magnificent torso was bare. She didn't dare imagine what he was—or wasn't—wearing on the lower half of his body.

He looked up from the device in his hand and, without taking his eyes from her, placed it on his bedside table.

Layla had never felt as self-conscious as she did during that walk to the bed. Not that self-conscious was the right phrasing for what she felt under the gleam of eyes that felt as if they were seeing straight through the kimono and cami to her naked skin.

Having reached her side of the bed, she sat awkwardly with her back to him and shrugged the robe off. Painfully aware that she had way more flesh on display than covered, even more aware that Sebastiano did too, she slipped under the sheets with her back to him.

The sheets rustled as Sebastiano made himself comfortable then the room was plunged into darkness.

Immediately the huge bed shrank.

She cocooned herself deeper into the sheets and fought to stop her airwaves closing up. The silence was so profound and Sebastiano so close he would surely be able to hear her erratic breaths.

His deep voice penetrated the silence. 'You did well with my family. I appreciate it must have been difficult for you.'

His voice was so close. *He* was so close.

Swallowing, she whispered, 'Your mother disapproves of me.'

His mother had been as gracious and welcoming as

the rest of the Russos but there had been an underlying stiffness that went beyond the stiffness that came from belonging to one of the richest families in the world. It was a stiffness that had felt personal.

'My mother would only have been happy if I was marrying a Sicilian.'

At least he wasn't denying it.

'You do realise your family know our marriage is all for show, right?' she said.

'They might suspect but they don't know.'

'Doesn't it bother you? All this lying?' And now she was a liar because of it too, and she would be lying in two days when she made her vows and lying with every display of affection she endured throughout the day...

But that in itself was a lie, she acknowledged. How could she call it *enduring* when she was tucked under the same bedsheets as him, intensely aware that if she slid her foot back just a few inches it would make contact with warm, hard flesh? Intensely aware that if Sebastiano moved just a few inches closer his breath would fall on her skin?

'Lies based on truth. Our marriage will be real for as long as it lasts, and my family will not question it because the only thing that matters is the bank's survival.'

'That all sounds very cold,' she managed to drag out as her pelvis contracted at the remembrance of how Sebastiano's lovemaking had been the antithesis of cold.

'To someone like you, perhaps.'

She rolled onto her back and turned her face to him without even thinking about it. 'Someone like *me*? What are you implying?'

Sebastiano gazed at her with eyes adjusted to the dark.

Even shadowed her beauty made his chest tighten in an echo of earlier, when he'd caught Layla's stare and lost the capacity to breathe. 'I am saying that I understand why my family and our priorities would seem cold to you. The nature of your relationship with your mother is very different from my relationship with my family.'

Her brow furrowed in question.

'I don't believe I have ever called my mother for the sake of calling her but you call yours frequently,' he explained. At least three times a day. The most recent had been only minutes ago. He'd stepped out of his bathroom and caught a hint of Layla's musical voice. It had been the softness in her tone that had been the giveaway as to who she was speaking to. It was a different kind of softness from the tone she took when speaking to her clients. With her mother, the softness had a chattier lilt; with her clients the softness was overlaid with the professionalism with which she spoke to her colleagues.

'I have an excellent relationship with my parents, but my personal life is private from them,' he continued. 'From what you've told me and what I've observed from your calls with her, you share confidences as if she was a close friend rather than your mother.'

Her gaze still locked on his, she turned her whole body to face him. Fingers appeared from beneath the sheets pulled up to her chin and her hand slid under her cheek. A long inhalation and then she quietly said, 'She's more than a mum to me. She's the closest friend I have.'

Curiosity had him ask, 'Do you think your closeness is because she raised you on her own?'

Her eyes narrowed a little in thought. 'That's definitely a factor, and her age when she had me was too.

She was so young and had no one to fall back on or tell her she was doing it wrong, so she had to trust her own instincts.' She gave the smallest of smiles. 'Basically, she made it up as she went along and did parenting her own way, and it was a way that meant we were always close.'

Her little finger was poking out at the side of her cheek. Sebastiano had the strangest urge to take it in his mouth and taste it.

Dio, he could still taste *her*. It was a taste that had lingered in his memories for all those months he'd spent determinedly refusing to think about her.

As he lay in the dark, each inhalation soaking in the sweetness of her breath and the last vestiges of her perfume, heady awareness thrummed heavily through him. That the awareness was shared and thrummed through Layla's veins too only heightened the sensation.

She'd been his for the taking earlier but that moment had passed. Her guard was up but different barriers had been lowered and their lowering was starting to satisfy a different kind of hunger, one he hadn't been aware had been roused.

A hunger to know everything about her.

'What do you mean by her *own way*?'

Her lips quirked with another small smile. 'Well…she never lectured for a start. When I was little and did anything naughty or plain wrong, she didn't sit in judgement. She would get me to talk about why I'd done whatever I'd done and steer me into realising why I'd been wrong to do it.' The smile curved a little wider. 'You could confess anything and her empathy and lack of judgement made you feel absolved but also a hundred times more guilty than if she'd got angry and ranted.'

'What did you do that was so bad?'

'That's just it—I didn't, not unless you count the time she caught me and my friend Natalie smoking when we were fourteen. She didn't lecture us on the evils of smoking, just gave us this awful, disappointed smile, kissed my head and told us to dispose of the butts responsibly. I don't know why it made us both feel so terrible but whatever witchcraft she used, it worked and neither of us ever touched a cigarette again. How can you rebel against someone like that? You can't…at least, I couldn't.'

'Your upbringing was very different from mine,' he told her slowly as he digested all she'd just confided and tried not to wonder what kind of mother Layla would be to the child he was finding it increasingly difficult to deny already existed inside her.

Difficult to deny but equally difficult to accept.

'I grew up knowing I wasn't just a member of a family but an institution,' he continued, forcing his thoughts back to safer ground. 'The bank has been in my family for five hundred years. I have known my whole life that my destiny is to lead it. My father knew it and his father before him, all the way back through the generations, but every family member plays their part in upholding the Russo image because all our fortunes depend on it and we marry accordingly. That is what I meant about my family not questioning our relationship—they know a background investigation will have been conducted on you because background investigations are always made on those we wish to bring into the fold through marriage. I appreciate that it sounds cold, but to us it is a necessary evil. It's survival. I do not have the luxury of allowing emotions to dictate my actions. None of us do.'

This was nothing Layla didn't already know through all the late nights in Sebastiano's suite, pouring his favourite bourbon, acting as a smiling sounding board for him. Many confidences had been shared with her, business and personal. In Sebastiano's case, business and personal were inextricably linked.

Now she was here, in his home, thrust into the heart of his world, she understood better the enormous pressure he was under. Understood it because she'd felt it, in his office when Sebastiano and his team had been waiting for the news about his monetary loss to drop. The tension had been like nothing she'd ever experienced, so tangible that it had felt like she could wave her fingers and find resistance in the air.

It was her own resistance she was having to hold onto now. The strange intimacy of a conversation in the still darkness.

He was so close that she could feel her pores opening to breathe him in, and, as hard as she tried, she was struggling to stop her gaze focusing on the sensuous mouth that had kissed every inch of her flesh. The urge to press a finger to the indentation on his bottom lip and then replace the finger with her mouth was so strong that she squeezed the pillow beneath her cheek even tighter and half joked, 'You don't have to explain yourself to me. I'm well aware you have the emotional range of a goldfish.'

And, when it came to women, the attention span of one too, she reminded herself.

Needed to remind herself, especially as her mild insult had resulted in a growl of surprised laughter that soaked straight into her open pores.

One night of bliss and Sebastiano had cast her aside. The emotional connection she thought she'd found in his arms hadn't existed for him.

'Being compared to a goldfish is an improvement on a pig,' he said musingly.

'You took pig to be a compliment.'

'But you meant it as an insult. You like goldfish.'

'How do you know that?' Surely a childhood pet goldfish wasn't the kind of thing an investigator would pick up?

His chuckle was husky, his voice smug. 'You just told me.'

She couldn't stop the snigger that escaped. 'If you're happy to be compared to a creature that only has the brain capacity to remember the last three seconds, then you do you.'

'I'm happy to be compared to a creature that you like.' His voice lowered. 'It gives me hope.'

It was the meaningful gleam in his eyes that finally gave Layla the impetus to roll over and turn her back to him.

It would be too easy to read something in his eyes that just wasn't there and hear false meaning in his words. Too easy to let herself forget how much he'd hurt her and give him the tools to do it again.

He was talking about sex. Nothing else.

She'd allowed herself to see and hear falsehoods in the dark of night with Sebastiano before. To him, they'd been just words. She'd been the fool for believing them.

Closing her eyes, she strove with everything she had to keep her voice light. 'Like I said, you do you. I'm going to get some sleep now, so time to stop talking.'

'Your wish is my command.'

She didn't know if she was breathing easier or harder when she felt him turn over and shift away, taking the warmth of his body with him.

There was movement as he made himself comfortable, and then he murmured her name.

She had to swallow to answer. 'Yes?'

'If I was to compare you to a creature it would be a swan. They're beautiful and elegant, just like you.'

Her chest expanded to accommodate her blooming heart, and she had to swallow even harder to speak. 'They also bite when provoked.'

His laughter rumbled through her skin. 'Kinky.'

She could have sobbed. 'Sebastiano?'

'Yes, my little rabbit?'

'Shut up and go to sleep.'

He gave one last husky chuckle and then silence finally fell.

The oblivion of sleep took many hours to claim her.

CHAPTER EIGHT

LAYLA KNEW SHE was alone in the bed before she even opened her eyes. Knew from the faint trace of cologne that Sebastiano had already showered and dressed. Knew from the all-consuming silence that he'd left the room.

She wouldn't see him again until they married. Russo family tradition dictated the bride and groom spent their day and night before a wedding apart.

A note had been placed on her bedside table. Rubbing the sleep from her eyes, she read, *I'll see you at the chapel tomorrow. Try not to miss me too much. S.*

Resting her head back on the pillow, she clutched the note to her chest and told herself the ache in her heart didn't mean she was missing him already.

Sebastiano had not expected to feel nerves. After the roller coaster of the last few weeks, he'd thought any nerves had been numbed but he stood at the altar of his chapel, colourfully dressed guests crammed into every available inch of space, his chest tight, stomach rolling, only half listening to what Paolo was chattering on about.

He had no reason to feel like this. Layla wasn't going to leave him stranded at the altar. Forget all she had to lose if she backed out, she just wouldn't do it. He knew it in his guts.

He supposed it was the twenty-four hours they'd spent apart giving time for doubt to sew its seeds.

He'd felt her absence acutely.

Five days in his home and it was like she'd imprinted into the walls. Every minute of their time apart had been spent with Layla lodged so firmly in his mind that he saw her everywhere.

She'd played her part beautifully. Everything was working out exactly as he'd intended. The fever for the wedding of the century was not just eclipsing the news about the money loss but putting it in so much shade that it was unlikely to ever see sunlight. It was the leading news story in all the Sicilian and Italian press, much of the rest of Europe's news channels including it in their coverage. An Italian television channel had set aside three hours of scheduling for an exclusive live feed of the wedding—negotiated by Sebastiano's people—which gave its crew access the press crammed at the villa gates could only dream about.

But what, he now wondered, would happen if sunlight ever did shine on the money loss? What would cause the press to dredge it back up? How long would he have to stay married to Layla for the press not to become suspicious of the timings? A few journalists were vocally doubting the veracity of the marriage but their columns and musings on the subject had been barely noticed, not when heads of state and industry had been congregating in Sicily with personal hairdressers and stylists joining them like additional baggage.

A few months of marriage would be too suspicious,

he now thought. To make it completely realistic, it would have to last a few years at the very least. And if Layla really was pregnant...

For the first time since the meal with his parents, he was unable to stop his mind from conjuring her hand absently resting on her stomach and the gentle stroke of her fingers.

Layla stepped out of the guest cottage, hardly able to believe how spectacular the grounds looked with all the imported pillars wrapped in blooming red and white roses surrounding the perimeter and the beautifully adorned benches, tables and chairs artfully placed throughout. With the beautiful, winged angel villa in the distance, the whole scene was like something out of a fairy tale. Her wedding dress made her feel like she was a character from a fairy tale. The horse drawn carriage that would take her through the vast estate to the chapel topped the fairy-tale feeling off.

Three footmen appeared. One held a hand out to her mother and helped her into the carriage. When he held out his hand for Layla, the other two carefully took the train of her dress and lifted it so she could sit without becoming entangled in it.

Holding tightly to her mum's hand, she did her best to compose her features into those of a typical excited bride for the video cameras strategically placed along the route for the live feed.

As much as she knew she shouldn't feel genuine excitement, she'd woken after a fitful night's sleep with butterflies in her stomach much like the ones she'd woken with as a child on her birthday. When the horses leading them trotted along the wide pathway that cut through Sebastiano's woodlands, overhung by arched trees, the butterflies grew in strength and her grip on her mother's hand tightened.

'It will all work out for the best,' her mum said quietly without dropping her smile. 'Have faith.'

Layla bit back from saying, *What, like it worked out for the best for you with my father?*

She wouldn't hurt her mother's feelings for the world.

As her mother had gently pointed out while they were holed up in the guest cottage, fate was already taking a different course from the one she'd had to follow when she was pregnant with Layla.

Sebastiano hadn't been wrong in his observation that mother and daughter were very different. Her mother trusted fate to make things right, even when it must have felt that fate was laughing at her. Layla trusted her fate and her baby's fate only in herself. Their marriage would make it impossible for Sebastiano to walk away from their child but she would not put faith in him being an involved father once they went their separate ways. She couldn't. The only people she could trust to love and cherish her baby were herself and her mother.

None of this stopped the butterflies flying up to her throat when the beautifully renovated ancient chapel appeared in the distance, the afternoon sun shining over its domed roof.

The footmen helped her down from the carriage and her bridesmaids, all Russo cousins and Russo cousins' children, took hold of the train.

Taking her mother's hand, Layla took the deepest breath of her life and walked through the open door.

Her heart burst into song to see the man waiting at the altar for her.

Sebastiano's laughter at Paolo's whispered observation that the fascinator being worn by a royal princess looked like a piece of plasticine 'art' his six-year-old daughter would make died on his lips as the vision from heaven appeared at the door.

A hush fell.

Stomach tightening, his pulses accelerated. Blood rushed to his head.

There was a dim awareness of music striking up. The heavenly vision's eyes locked onto his and then even the music ceased to exist for him.

Slowly, she glided to him like a shimmering wingless angel. Her figure-hugging white dress with its spaghetti sleeves and scooped neckline that skimmed her cleavage was embellished with thousands of tiny crystals, around her swanlike neck a large teardrop blue-diamond necklace, smaller matching earrings on display, her hair swept into a side knot.

And then she smiled her perfect lopsided smile and the angel vanished and sexy, beautiful Layla, all warm flesh and hot blood, took her place. In an instant the blood pounding in his head fell into his expanding heart, and he took her hand from the woman beside her...her mother...and drew her to him.

Dio, he'd known she would be the most beautiful bride to have ever graced Sicily's soil but even he hadn't imagined such a magical vision.

'You are spellbinding,' he breathed into her ear, and was rewarded with another dazzling lopsided smile.

Fingers threaded, they faced the priest and the wedding mass began.

When Layla had first been told Sebastiano had organised a full Catholic wedding ceremony, she'd wondered how she would make it through a whole hour without yawning or fidgeting, but the magic of it all had seeped into her from her first look at her groom. As the ceremony went on, the music, the singing, the candles, the incense, even the Italian it was all conducted in, all commingled and slipped silently into her soul and filled it with light.

This was *her* marriage. Sebastiano was *her* groom. Her groom, looking as handsome as she'd ever seen him in a full morning suit complete with light grey waistcoat and dark grey silk cravat and handkerchief. A proper groom. A proper groom for a proper wedding.

In that moment it came to her that whatever their reasons for marrying and whatever happened in the future, their marriage for however long it lasted would be real. Everything else, from Sebastiano's reputation escaping untarnished and his ancient bank continuing with a Russo at the helm, even her law firm thriving on the money he'd be pumping into it, was a side-effect to the two most potent truths. They would be husband and wife, and their child, whatever denial Sebastiano might currently be experiencing, would have a father. A real father who, once he accepted the truth, would want it.

It was time to make their vows.

Hands clasped, they faced each other.

The priest addressed Sebastiano first. His lips moved in response but Layla's head was too full to hear.

How many brides pledged their lives to a man only to find their hearts shattered when the true nature of their loves finally came out? she wondered.

She already knew Sebastiano's true nature and because she knew it, he could never shatter her heart. He'd already done his worst. He'd lied to her. Ghosted her. Blackmailed her. Forced her into this marriage. Denied their child. She wouldn't count kidnap seeing as she'd started that part by cuffing him to a bed, but, if not for that, she could add kidnapping to her list of wrongs.

None of that meant their marriage had to be a nightmare to live through, not unless she chose to make it so.

He wouldn't make it a nightmare for her. He could. Easily. But he wouldn't. It was a certainty she felt all the way to her marrow.

The priest turned to her and recited her vows in English.

She gazed into the green depths of Sebastiano's eyes. Caught the glimmer of desire that was never far from the surface.

Caught something else too. A steadfast openness.

The little avocado-sized life in her belly stirred. Just a little fluttering before stilling again, but it was enough to make her already expanded heart bloom further as she kept her stare on the father of the little life and said, with only the slightest hitch in her voice, 'I do.'

Sebastiano stood with his new wife in the back garden of his estate shaking hands with the guests lined up to congratulate them. The train of her dress had been cleverly removed, champagne and canapés were circulating, background music playing, conversations being struck between friends and strangers alike, children running wild and letting off steam after the long service. All of this he registered on a subconscious level.

His lips still burned from the kiss they'd shared to seal their marriage. And the kiss they'd shared for the official wedding photos. His neck still burned from the cup of her hand to it when she'd leaned in for those kisses. His loins still burned from the effect of the glimmer fired at him from her forget-me-not eyes in the beat before their mouths had fused.

The line had shortened considerably when Laurence and his husband reached them. After vigorously shaking Sebastiano's hand and thanking him profusely for flying the entire firm over and putting them up in a nearby hotel for the weekend, he pulled Layla into an enormous bear hug.

'Aren't you the dark horse?' He beamed when he released her from his embrace. Holding her biceps, he stared at her with the pride of a father. 'Not even a hint that you were seeing this fine fellow.'

'We wanted to keep it private until we were both certain,' she said without missing a beat.

'Well, I'm delighted for you. We all are. And what a glorious home. You'll never drag yourself back to London.'

'Just watch me,' she said, laughing. 'I'll be back at my desk in three weeks. You'll never get rid of me.'

'Exactly what I wanted to hear!'

Once the line dwindled to nothing it was time to circulate properly with the people who most needed to be satisfied that Russo Banca Internazionale remained in safe hands. Layla remained glued to his side, holding conversations with the spouses who wanted to know all about her. The moment Layla told the spouses about her firm, the partners tuned in too, their interest piqued. Whatever their charitable public personas might say, it was beyond most of their guests' comprehension that anyone could spend all those years in education to choose a career with a law firm that barely paid a living wage.

By the time the gong rang out informing the wedding party it was time for the wedding feast, Layla had taken so much of the spotlight with their guests that he doubted any of them gave another thought about Sebastiano other than to think he must be the luckiest man in Europe to have snared such a beautiful, intelligent, compassionate wife. He'd even overheard his mother telling a group of her society friends that, though she was of course disappointed Layla wasn't Sicilian, she was perfect in every other way.

'Nicely played,' he murmured as they headed inside to the banquet room.

She squeezed her fingers threaded through his and smiled.

'Extra nice touch pointing Laurence out to them all.' The donations would come flooding in, he was certain.

'I thought so too,' she said beatifically, then winked and added, 'I'm still holding you to that five million you promised the firm, though.'

'I will transfer it first thing in the morning,' he assured her.

She stopped walking and, eyes brimming with glee, tapped the end of his nose. 'Exactly what I wanted to hear.'

He captured her hand and kissed it. 'You seem happy.'

She radiated with it, a glow emanating from her that dazzled.

She laughed softly. 'I'm an excellent actress, remember?'

If this happiness was an act then it was the performance of her life.

Slipping an arm around her waist, he pulled her flush to him. 'Can you act the role of bride who can't bear to wait another second without a kiss from her new husband?'

'Let me see…' She cupped the back of his neck and raised her face to his. He breathed in the scent of her sweet breath before her lips brushed as lightly as a feather to his. With a sigh, she tilted her head back and gazed into his eyes. 'How was that?'

He gave a soft growl. 'You call that a kiss?'

'I call it an aperitif.'

Damn it, but there was a pull in his loins, the telltale tugs of arousal manifesting into something physical.

Instead of doing the sane thing and letting her go, he held her even more tightly to him. 'An aperitif or a tease?'

Eyes gleaming, her teeth razed against her bottom lip. And then she kissed him properly, a deep, hungry kiss that filled his senses with her sweet taste and made him wish for a trapdoor to fall through with her and a soft mattress to land on.

He didn't know which of them broke it, but when they came apart, her cheeks were so flushed and her eyes so dazed that he knew this part, at least, was no act.

Hands still hooked around his neck, she cleared her throat and whispered, 'Better?'

Worse. Much worse. Unless he let her go right now,

he'd never be able to show his face in polite society again. 'That was an upgrade on the aperitif,' he conceded.

Exhaling a sigh, she unhooked her arms, stepped back and rubbed her thumb against the side of his mouth. Then she smiled her beautiful lopsided smile and teased, 'We can't have Sebastiano Russo dining with world leaders with lipstick around his mouth, can we?'

Layla felt giddy as she danced with her new husband and swathes of their guests on the magnificent dancefloor. She kept expecting someone to pinch her and wake her from this dream where her favourite singer in the world was performing on the ballroom stage at *her* wedding.

She couldn't begin to think of the effort and cost—and headache—it had taken for Sebastiano to fly the world's most famous diva over at such short notice. And he'd done it for her. All because of a passing comment Layla had once made when selecting music for him to listen to in his suite, which made her think back to the two occasions guests at the parties he'd thrown in his suite had made drunken lewd comments to her. He'd kicked the offenders out without ceremony and with a sincere apology to her. She'd never seen those men again. Neither of them were here at the wedding.

He must have been close to them to have invited them to those parties, she now realised. All the other men who'd attended were here. One of them was dancing next to Sebastiano, shouting over the music something he clearly wasn't listening to because his gaze was fixed on her.

It was a gaze that never failed to make her heart skip and her pulses race.

* * *

Sebastiano rarely danced at social gatherings that were more public than private. He'd assumed he'd dance the traditional first dance with Layla and then network with his more distinguished guests, but nearly two hours on, he was still there. Still moving his body in beat to the music, too entranced with the graceful beauty who'd taken centre stage without even realising it to want to move away from her. The graceful beauty who was now his wife.

He'd caught the singer narrowing her eyes at the bride and was certain the diva wouldn't think twice about scratching Layla's eyes out for taking all the attention away from her. From the wide smile on his beautiful bride's face, she was oblivious to her heroine's maleficent thoughts, and as he watched her sing along to her heroine's lyrics with her mother, Sebastiano thought for the first time of the one person missing from the celebrations. Layla's father.

He thought back to her mother being the one to walk Layla down the aisle, remembered the huge, almost familial embrace Layla and Laurence had shared earlier.

Her father had been mentioned only once between them, when Sebastiano himself had carelessly thrown his abandonment as an attribute for people to admire her overcoming.

His eyes dipped down to her stomach and that tugging sensation hit him again, stronger than it had ever done before.

A new, slower song started.

She turned to face him and without missing a beat— Layla *never* missed a beat—she hooked her arms around his neck and gazed into his eyes with an expression that vanquished the tugging sensation, a deeper, more sensuous tugging taking its place.

'Enjoying the party?' she asked softly.

'Very much.' Much more than he'd ever believed he would enjoy his own wedding. Whenever he'd envisaged it, he'd imagined the bride being one of the women who inhabited his society, a woman who didn't need to put on a performance to fit into his world. A woman who bored him to tears.

His real marriage would be as transactional as his marriage to Layla, a union much like his parents had, built on mutual respect solely to produce an heir. He'd always assumed that once the requisite heir—and preferably a few spares—had been produced, then he would follow the tradition of his world and take a mistress and his wife take a lover, any and all affairs conducted with the utmost discretion.

The transactional nature of his marriage to Layla was as different from any future marriage as night from day, Layla herself as different from any future bride as the sun was from the moon.

If his growing conviction that she was indeed pregnant…

No. This was not the time to think of it. Not here. Not now. Not when he had her in his arms and the look in her eyes was telling him she didn't want to be anywhere else.

'You?' he added.

She pretended to consider it. 'I've been to worse.'

He grinned and, because he could, tightened his hold

around her and kissed her, ignoring propriety to deepen it until she broke it with another of those breathless sighs that only fed his need for her.

CHAPTER NINE

As much as Sebastiano wanted to throw Layla over his shoulder, whisk her upstairs and lock the bedroom door, a tendril of the propriety he'd come within a breath of losing completely reasserted itself.

He was not a hormonal schoolboy. He was the head of Russo Banca Internazionale. His bank and his place in it were the whole reason he'd married her...with a dollop of revenge thrown in. When it came down to it, this marriage was a performance and though he knew damned well that Layla was as caught in the web of desire as he was, he could not say with any certainty whether she would act on it in the privacy of the bedroom or switch it off.

As he was learning, what Layla's mouth said didn't always correspond with what her eyes said. As he was also learning, it was her eyes that always told the truth. If he'd recognised the steel in the forget-me-nots the night she'd tricked five million pounds out of him, he'd have recognised that something was very wrong. Instead, he'd been too caught up in the desire that had also pulsed in them and the soft musicality of her voice and the glimpses of cleavage, too damned arrogant and confident in his own greatness to think of the hurt he'd caused her at his failure to call. At disappearing from her life.

Despite knowing it might all come to nothing, by the time he'd taken to the stage to thank the singer and all their guests, then fought through the crowd wanting to wish them, again, a long and happy marriage, another hour had passed and the heat of his desire had barely lowered by a degree.

He'd have to sleep in his bathroom. Lock the door, fill the bath with cold water and submerge himself in it.

And so, even though Layla's hand was firmly clasped in his as they climbed the stairs together, Sebastiano concentrated only on filling his lungs with air.

Their hands slipped apart at the door.

His heart beating harder and faster than it ever had before, he took a deep, deep breath, followed her inside and rested his back against the wall.

After the noise of the ballroom, the silence in the bedroom was absolute. He had a vague awareness of rose petals making a path to the bed and the rose-petal hearts created on the turned-down sheets, but it was just a background blur to the main picture before him.

Layla. Staring at him with colour heightening her cheeks, so ravishingly beautiful it made his heart hurt to look at her, standing close enough for the scent of her heated skin beneath the remnants of her sultry perfume to snake into his airwaves. Close enough for him to see the pulse beating at the base of her neck. Close enough for him to hear the unevenness of her breaths.

Dio, he'd never known his own breaths to be so heavy. Everything in him felt weighty, as if desire had been injected into his veins.

Layla's body had forgotten how to breathe.

The dreamlike quality the day had taken since her revelation in the church and the glowing hours that had passed since had vanished under the weight of the choice she had to make and under the headier weight of the desire burning in every cell of her body and the blaze of Sebastiano's hunger in the depths of his eyes.

Their night together had been passionate, hedonistic perfection. Sebastiano had drawn something out of her she'd never even suspected existed, something that had destroyed all her inhibitions from the first sweep of their tongues.

When they'd parted the next morning, she'd felt the wrench of his absence a hundred times more acutely than she'd ever done for Chris. A thousand times more.

Three years she'd been with Chris and she hadn't shed a single tear when it ended. He'd been safe, she now realised. He'd been content to wait all those months for her to share his bed, something she'd only gone ahead with in the end because she'd felt she owed it to him for all his patience.

Sebastiano was the antithesis of safe. She'd known that from the moment she first set eyes on him. She'd only slept with him that night because she'd set out thinking it would only *be* for that one night. She'd thought she was safe.

She'd had no idea when she stepped into his arms that their one night together would leave in her a mark that ran deeper than the child they'd conceived. No idea that his subsequent ghosting of her would leave her desolate.

But history didn't have to repeat itself. That was something she'd told herself over and over when she'd learned she was pregnant. Her mother's path did not have to be hers. She'd taken control to stop that very thing from happening, and she'd healed and fortified her heart.

The stark truth, though, was that Sebastiano brought her to life in a way she'd never felt before. He hadn't just drawn a hidden sexuality out of her but a passionate fire that blazed in all its forms whenever she was with him. With Sebastiano, all her senses came alive.

And now her eyes were wide open.

And so were his. While electricity crackled like white noise between them, his unfaltering gaze remained steady.

She understood the silent message he was sending.

He would not touch her.

He'd made a promise that here, in the sanctity of their bedroom, it was for Layla to make the first move and he would hold himself to it. If she turned away from him he would do nothing to stop her.

Staring into his pulsing green eyes, soaking the barely contained hunger emanating from them, it came to her in a flash of wonder that just as their marriage would only be a nightmare if she made it so, Sebastiano could only hurt her again if she let him...

Her feet left the ground before the rest of her knew what she was doing.

She moved so quickly and so suddenly that Sebastiano barely had the time to register what was happening before Layla's arms wound tightly around his neck and her lips compressed to his with a soft yet wrenching moan.

The relief was almost as strong a sensation as the blood that pumped after that long heart-stopping moment when he'd detected a frisson of fear in the depths of the forget-me-nots.

Whatever doubts or fears had caught her in those moments were gone, her mouth as hot and hungry as his own, her fingers digging into his skull as urgently as his bit into her back. The need to taste and feel every inch of her swept through him like its own life force.

Deeper and harder their mouths moved together, tongues exploring ravenously, his senses feeding on the exotic, sensually sweet taste that had sat in him like a hidden memory waiting for the trigger to reawaken it. And Layla was the trigger. Layla, shedding the cloak of hurt his actions had forced her to wrap herself in for protection and embracing the desire that had flickered between them for so very long and which their night together had turned into a flame.

Why had he run from that flame in the aftermath? he wondered dimly as he buried his face in her neck and resisted the heady urge to bite down. No one made him feel like this. No one. Only Layla. No one else had ever made him ache to burrow himself into their skin. No one else had fingers that could slide down his neck and send sensation coursing to the tips of his toes.

Her breath hot and ragged in his hair, those same fingers now dragged over his chest to tug at his shirt and pull it free. His arousal deepened when she scraped her nails through the hair on his abdomen before fumbling at the button of his trousers.

In thrilling frustration at being unable to find the zip or button or whatever the hell it was holding her wedding dress together, he spun her around and pressed her against the wall to keep her steady, then clasped either side of the seam running from beneath her shoulder blades to the base of her spine, and pulled with all his strength.

Layla gasped to hear the loud rip of her beautiful dress and the shock of cold wall against fevered skin that had moments before been covered, the gasp turning into a moan when Sebastiano's mouth and teeth grazed her shoulder as he pinched the spaghetti sleeves and yanked them down her arms. The top part of the dress fell and bunched at her waist.

The fever in her was more than skin deep. It had sunk into her veins and bones, burning even the tips of her fingers working frantically to undo the button of his trousers and release the bulging hardness trapped beneath the silky material. With the shackles of her fears finally thrown off, her desperation for Sebastiano's possession had mushroomed, all the desire she'd been suppressing unleashed and seeking the possession of the only man in the world to make her feel whole and complete.

His trousers finally unbuttoned, she yanked at the zip and reached inside the tight confines of his briefs. His groan of pleasure and biting kiss when she wrapped her fingers around his throbbing excitement only fed the burn of her own arousal.

'*Dio*, Layla,' he muttered into her mouth before scraping his stubbly cheek against hers, tugging again at her dress, trying to rip it at the waist, and mumbling something unintelligibly Italian that was an aphrodisiac all of its own whatever the words meant.

Everything about Sebastiano was an aphrodisiac to Layla, from his voice and accent to the musky taste and scent of his skin to the silkiness of his hair. She wanted to touch and taste him everywhere, feel his touch and taste everywhere, had never hated clothes more.

It was a hate frustrating Sebastiano as much as her, his efforts to rip away the multiple layers of the skirt of her dress proving impossible. With a loud growl, he lifted her into his arms and practically threw her onto the bed.

In moments he was straddling her thighs and with the same strength he'd torn the back of her dress, he pulled at his waistcoat. Buttons went flying, pinging as they landed on the hardwood floor but she barely heard them, too intent on hooking her arm around his neck for more rousing, heady kisses. Before he'd come into her life she'd never known kissing could evoke such thrills, could be so addictive.

With her free hand she yanked at the buttons of his shirt, shivering with pleasure as he undid her strapless white lace bra, then cried out loud when he covered her breast with his mouth and lathered it with such pleasure that the burn between her legs became molten. Such was her need that when the buttons of his shirt remained stubbornly unbuttoned, she found a strength she'd never known she possessed and, following his lead, ripped it open.

The moment their chests pressed together, a tiny part of the fever burning through her abated, as if her skin had been so desperate to feel his flesh upon it that it gave a little sigh of relief. The sigh lasted only a moment. The relief she so desperately sought was a wedding dress away and, lips fusing back together with his, she kicked at the thick layers entangled around her legs and feet; could have wept when Sebastiano roughly gathered together as much of it as he could and pulled it up to her waist.

His large hand ran over her thigh and he groaned into her mouth when he found the top of her white lace hold-up, and when he slid a finger into the side of her knickers and found her wet and swollen for him, his hooded eyes widened and nostrils flared. *'La mia carne brucia ti desidero da morire,'* he said raggedly before his mouth fused back to hers.

The pleasure of his fingers caressing her where she so desperately craved had her crying into his mouth and clamping her thighs together and when he slid another finger inside her she rocked into him before crying with frustration when he moved his hand and ripped her knickers apart.

Her cries of frustration became cries of anticipation when he pushed the material of her dress up some more and yanked his trousers and briefs down to free himself properly. At the first tantalising hint of his arousal jabbing against her inner thigh she spread her legs wider and lifted her bottom, every inch of her body begging for his possession. Her breaths coming in short pants, she tightened her hold around his neck as he fought his way through the mass of material stubbornly keeping them apart until, finally, magically, he drove deep inside her.

Such was the sensation that all the air flew out of her with a moan of the deepest pleasure.

Their mouths broke apart as he lifted his head back to gaze wonderingly into her eyes. She could feel the throbs of his arousal inside her, knew he could feel the throbs of her own as her needy body adjusted to the most glorious sensation of Sebastiano filling it so completely.

But it was the swirling pulses in his green eyes, which had darkened to look almost black, that had her lift her face back to him and kiss him with all the passion in her singing heart.

With a ragged groan against her lips, he clasped hold of her bottom and in moments every fibre of her being was singing in sensation.

Sebastiano was beyond thoughts. Beyond savouring the moment. They were both beyond that. They both needed relief and with Layla's long legs wrapped around him, her moans and breathless cries urging him on with the same urgency as the nails digging in his back, he drove in and out of her like a man possessed…he *was* a man possessed…possessing *her* and making her his with every hard thrust…

Dio, this was something else. Something unimaginable, something that went beyond being bare inside her. It was all he could do to hold on until her breaths shortened and she began to rock against him. Only when he felt the thickening around his arousal that had blown his mind all those months ago did he let himself go with a roar before he was pulled deep, deep into the secret place that belonged only to him and Layla.

Layla's eyes were closed, her hands gripping the pillow tightly as the sensations being evoked by Sebastiano's tongue deepened and her climax built into a crescendo.

Only when she'd finally stilled did he lift his head from between her legs and give his lascivious smile. 'Better?'

Finally too replete to speak, she smiled and held her arms out to him in answer. In response, he crawled back up and placed his head on the pillow beside her. Kissing her gently, he slung an arm over her stomach.

She gazed into his eyes and nuzzled her face closer. 'Sure you don't want me to return the favour?'

He laughed lowly and kissed her again. 'Soon. You, my insatiable little rabbit, have worn me out.'

She grinned sleepily. 'Worth it?'

Another kiss. 'Completely.'

The first filters of daylight were coming through the heavy drapes. They hadn't slept a wink. The bedroom looked like a romantic bomb had gone off. Rose petals, buttons and the tiny crystals of her wedding dress were strewn all over the floor along with puddles of their torn, ruined clothes. She didn't dare think how much money's worth of bespoke clothing they'd destroyed in their desperation to be skin on skin.

She didn't want to think, either, of how similar their wedding night had been to their first night together. Once hadn't been enough then either. Twice hadn't been enough. Three times hadn't been enough.

Sebastiano had ended up having to cut the wedding dress off her. The zip had stuck fast and the layers of the skirt were just too thick and heavy to rip through. He'd taken one look at her naked—excepting her white lace hold-ups—and she'd taken one look at him looking at her and before she knew it he'd been buried deep inside her again. Only on their third bout, after they'd shared a shower together, had they taken it more slowly. After their fourth time, this time while sharing another shower, she'd hardly been able to walk. She'd been astounded when, shortly after, back in bed, laughing about some of the fascinators their guests had worn while he'd idly encircled her breast with his fingers, desire had flamed back to life.

Finally, after her fifth orgasm of the night, Layla's desire had muted into a gentle simmer...for now.

For a long time, they just lay there, Layla on her back with her face to him, Sebastiano on his side, his eyes closed, only the gentle circles he was now making on her stomach signs he was still awake.

'Can you feel it?' she whispered. The fluttery feeling had started again, right beneath his hand.

Sebastiano's eyes flew open, the sleepiness he'd been falling into shaking off him in an instant.

Layla's open stare was glued to him.

She caught the hand frozen on her stomach and pressed it down. 'It feels like a thick fluttering. It's like no other feeling in the world. My body's changed so little that sometimes I worry I'm imagining the whole thing but it's real and it's there. That's our baby.'

Blood roared in his ears. The tugging sensation every time he looked at her belly was stronger than it had ever been, and now, with his hand splayed on it and his full concentration on the sensation beneath his skin, he could feel the strange fullness of it. The changes that came with a belly supporting the creation of a life.

'Yes,' he admitted quietly. 'I can feel it.'

He could deny it to himself no more. Layla was pregnant.

She expelled a soft breath of relief.

'But how can it be mine? We used protection the whole time.' Every time. Which only reaffirmed that, subconsciously, he'd already accepted the truth of the pregnancy because he hadn't given protection a thought earlier.

There was a helpless quality to her smile. 'I know we did and I can't explain it either but this baby is yours. There was only one man before you and that ended when I graduated.'

Just the thought of her being with anyone else punched nausea through him.

Stifling it, he rolled onto his back and gazed at the ceiling. 'I want to believe it's mine but how can I? I accept that accidents happen but nothing went wrong with the condoms.' Nothing at all. For sure, their night together had been the most intense and passionate of his life...until tonight, that was...but he'd been meticulous in his protection of them both.

At her silence, he turned his face back to her and saw the unshed tears swimming in her eyes. It was a sight that made his chest tighten immeasurably, and he found himself saying, 'It doesn't matter who the father is.'

As part of his investigation into Layla he'd had his team dig into her lovers. The only name to come up had been from her university years. He'd also got them to do a forensic account of her movements for the two months either side of their night together. Whoever the real father was, there was no proof of his existence but that didn't mean he could accept that he'd created the child with her. Sebastiano was a Catholic who didn't believe in miracles.

'The whole point of the marriage was to avoid a scandal,' he continued. 'The child will have my name and the world will see it as mine.'

Covering her breasts with the bedsheets, she sat up and stared down at him. Unshed tears still glistened but he could see her thinking hard. 'Why would you force this marriage on me if you didn't believe you were the father? I know you've been in denial but you must know it deep down else why put those clauses about children *born* within the marriage in our prenup? Why not make the clauses state conception?'

A flare of anger ignited. 'I told you, this marriage has to be believable to everyone and it's already proving to be—the wedding has eclipsed the monetary loss, and when news of the pregnancy breaks it will only add to the momentum. As for the prenup, it was drafted by the legal firm who have taken care of my family's personal business for nearly as long as Russo Banca has been operational. It is unthinkable for a man in my position to not have one and it would have been unthinkable to write conception into the clause. That is the kind of thing that makes people ask questions.'

She shook her head in disbelief. 'You accept that I'm pregnant. You've had me thoroughly investigated. You *know* there's been no one else and yet you *still* refuse to believe you're the father?'

'I don't believe in miracles, Layla,' he said tightly. 'I believe in tangible facts, but the child's paternity makes no difference to me. I set us on the path to marriage knowing there was a slim possibility that you were pregnant with another man's child—'

'It's *yours*,' she stated vehemently.

'A discreet paternity test after the birth will confirm that.'

A flash of pain lit her beautiful features at this.

'You're not worried about the imaginary father coming out of the woodwork?' she asked.

Sebastiano took a deep breath to douse the last of his anger. He didn't want what had been a spectacular day to end in an argument and bad feeling. As much as he enjoyed verbally sparring with Layla and seeing her passion roused in all its forms, this felt different from their previous sparrings. Or was his acceptance that she really was pregnant making him feel different about it?

'If it happens, he will be dismissed as a fantasist,' he said in a gentler tone, turning back to face her. 'Whatever happens, the child will be raised as mine.'

She slumped back down and held herself rigidly, chin jutted, her mouth clamped in a thin line. 'You had this all planned out, didn't you?'

Not planned but dealt with in his mind and filed away to be used only if needed.

'I never leave things to chance.' He moved closer and wrapped an arm around her. 'You should be pleased.'

Her eyes flashed, the anger he'd rid himself of transferred to her.

He kissed her smooth shoulder. 'You win whatever happens, and so does your child.' Pinching the bedsheets tucked so tightly under her arms, he pulled them down to expose her small but perfectly formed breasts, and cupped one, capturing a nipple between his fingers. 'He or she will have a recognised father and security for life. That is what you wanted for them, isn't it, when you chained me to that bed and demanded money?'

Her mutinous expression remained but her body, responding to his touch, spoke a completely different language.

Carefully sliding on top of her, he smoothed the hair from her face and watched the forget-me-nots pulse when his arousal jutted against her pubis. 'I know I forced this marriage on you, *cara*, but I don't want you to be unhappy and I don't want us to be at war. Believe me when I tell you that I will do everything in my power to be a good father to the life inside you.'

Layla gazed into the green depths and, with a deep sigh that came from her heart, palmed his cheek. He nuzzled into it, which only made the sigh in her heart deepen.

It frightened her how badly his continued denial about being the father hurt. It meant he was denying *her*. Meant he believed she was capable of passing off another man's child as his.

But he was trying to do the right thing and that counted for something. His honesty counted for something too. If she let his denial fester then the only person she hurt would be herself.

Lifting her thighs so his arousal pressed right where they both most wanted it to be, she brought her mouth up to his and whispered, 'I don't want to be at war either.'

His lips lifted at the corners. 'Then let us make peace,' he said huskily before fusing his mouth to hers and, with a long, drawn-out groan, drove deep inside her.

CHAPTER TEN

THE ISLAND SEBASTIANO flew them to for their honeymoon was everything Layla had anticipated.

Entirely private, the golden beach lapped at their villa's flowering front lawn. The skeleton staff was even more skeleton than she'd imagined, a husband-and-wife team who lived in a small cottage at the rear of the grounds and who only came to the villa when they were called for.

The honeymoon clothes that had been brought ahead for her were exactly as she'd imagined, mostly consisting of string bikinis and scraps of lace that called itself lingerie. She didn't bother with any of it, preferring to drive Sebastiano insane by wearing various skimpy, strappy little summer dresses and absolutely nothing underneath. If she wanted to swim or sunbathe, she simply threw it off and paraded around naked.

It was the most liberating feeling in the world, almost as liberating as having sex whenever and wherever she wanted. Or whenever or wherever Sebastiano wanted.

After four days, there wasn't an item of furniture in the whole villa they hadn't had sex on or against. She could no longer walk into the kitchen without her pelvis throbbing to remember how she'd been pouring herself a glass of water when he'd sneaked up behind her and bent her over the work surface. She could no longer walk past the swimming pool without seeing the sun longue he'd been laid back on, dozing, when she'd woken him by taking him in her mouth.

Sometimes it shocked her, how she had absolutely no inhibitions with Sebastiano. None at all. It didn't matter how many times she climaxed. Still she wanted more. And more. And more.

More of him. Constantly.

She was self-aware enough to know that constant love-making meant she didn't have to think too deeply about anything other than making love. It didn't change that here on this beautiful, dreamily romantic island, she was little more than a receptacle for pleasure, that her insides turned to fire just to look at him.

Wasn't all this what she'd told herself the day she'd made her vows? That their marriage only had to be a nightmare if she chose to make it so? That Sebastiano could only hurt her again if she let him? Hadn't they both agreed that they didn't want their marriage to be a war?

And so she'd chosen to push aside the wrench in her heart at his denial of paternity and concentrate on the one thing that was always good between them. After all, she'd made those vows without any illusions, and in a way he had a point, that she should be happy her baby would have the security she'd always craved.

When they parted ways, Sebastiano would already have the proof of paternity he insisted on and her child would have what she'd never had. Financial security *and* a father.

And just in case he did renege on it and found a way

to overturn their prenup, she had the suburban house to fall back on.

Until they parted ways, or overdosed on lovemaking, whichever came first, she had a lover, which was what she was training herself to see him as. Her lover.

If she kept thinking of him as her husband then she risked the danger of believing it.

Sebastiano kept expecting to wake from the dream he'd fallen into. He'd always had a high sex drive but this was something else. Five days of pure hedonism and now he was being ridden by Layla on the outside dining chair, her breast in his mouth and her hair covering them both like a sheet. The sun was setting over the sea, the sky a dark orange, the heady perfume of flowers in the air around them but losing to the sultry fragrance and taste of Layla.

He could not get enough of her. If sex was an addiction then he was rapidly becoming addicted to having sex with her. He probably already was addicted.

Who knew, he wondered, dazed after yet another powerful climax, that it was possible to become addicted to sex with your own wife?

He was still inside her when she kissed him and murmured, 'Shower, my lover?'

He laughed gruffly, thinking of the untouched plates on the table beside them. 'Food, then shower?'

She blinked as if she'd forgotten all about the meal they'd been about to share then brightened. 'Oh, yes! Food.' One last kiss and she climbed off him.

It was as she scooped her discarded dress off the patio

tiles and pulled it over her head that he saw it. The slight bump of her belly.

When had *that* appeared? And had her breasts grown...?

'What's wrong?'

He met the questioning forget-me-nots and shook his head. 'Nothing. Just thinking how beautiful you are.'

She blushed and smiled and retook the rattan seat she'd been on before she'd pounced on him. Helping herself to a chip, she chewed on it then jumped back to her feet. 'Music?'

Pulling his shorts up, he laughed and reached for a chip of his own. Layla was never happier than when music was playing...apart from when making love, that was. His addiction to having sex with Layla was completely mutual. 'Sure.'

But, sitting back down and watching her fiddle with her phone to connect her playlist with the villa's outdoor speakers, he found his gaze drawn again to her stomach and breasts. His thudding heart felt colder than the chip that had stuck in his throat. Even though her short dress was floaty, he could see the delineation of a stomach that had seemingly swollen over the space of an hour. For the first time, he could *see* that she was pregnant.

Jazz music piped out. He dragged his stare away from her stomach to her face.

She tapped his nose and grinned. 'Got you.'

A moment later a band they both like replaced it and she sat back down. After she'd piled her plate with salad and a handful more of the cold chips, her forehead creased with concern. 'Are you sure there's nothing wrong?'

What could he tell her? That her pregnancy was showing and his heart had turned cold for it?

Had it turned cold? Or had that just been his chest? Was there a difference?

He wished he could erase the cynicism that stopped him from believing in anything that wasn't tangible and verifiable. When his mind refused to see Layla with another man was it because his current addiction to her had made her so entirely his or because he wanted to believe the baby could be his too much?

And that was where the danger lay. *How* could he believe? He'd thought about that night so many times and there was not a single moment when he'd been careless.

But why would she lie? What was there to gain by it when she already had the money, he'd paid Laurence the money for the firm and she'd been promised a minimum of a further fifty million? She could walk away now and he'd be obliged to give it to her.

She had no need to lie. Not now.

So why couldn't he make the leap of faith in either his head or his heart?

He opened his mouth to assure her again that nothing was wrong, then changed his mind before the words formed, instead asking, 'How did you become so good at acting?'

The crease in her forehead became one of confusion.

'You're one person one minute and someone else the next. You can turn it on like a tap.'

'But you do the same,' she protested, clearly taken aback. 'Everyone does. How we are together... When we're alone you're almost a different man from how you are in your professional life.'

'I get your point but my professional persona and who I am when it's just you and me, they are still just me. I cannot assimilate into being someone else like you can. I knew you for two years and you gave no hint that you were anything more than a bar tender.'

'You never asked.'

'I appreciate that, but you never showed a side of yourself that would make me question that there was more to you than what you were showing.'

'I was being what you wanted from a bar tender.'

'And that is *my* point. You are a chameleon. I can only be different versions of myself but you can assimilate into being whoever you want or whatever you think someone wants you to be. You have slotted into my life and family as if you were born into Sicilian society—'

'But that's what you wanted me to do! It's partly why you made me marry you!'

He took a deep breath to keep his tone calm. 'I'm not denying that but I want to understand how you do it. I want to understand where it comes from. I want to understand *you*, Layla.'

She gave a helpless shrug. 'I don't know where it comes from. It's not something I think about.'

'What is it then? Some kind of super power?' He was only half joking. Sebastiano had met plenty of actors and actresses in his time, many of them award winning. If Layla was on a stage with them she would act them off it.

Shoving her chair back a little, she drew her knees up and wrapped her arms around her calves. 'I honestly don't know.' A short shake of her head. 'I've never thought about it.'

'Try this then—when can you first remember doing it?'

Clearly upset, she sucked her cheeks in and grazed her bottom lip. 'Primary school,' she eventually replied. 'I realised very quickly that I was different from the other children, and I didn't want to be different.'

'What made you different from them?'

'What do you think?' She shook her head. 'I was the only one without a father.'

'There must have been other children growing up in single-parent homes.'

'Yes, but I was the only one who had literally never met the other parent. I can remember, very distinctly, re-alising that I was the only child in my class who didn't know their father, and begging my mum to let me meet him. I thought she could magic him up for me.' Her lips pulled in and she swallowed. 'Looking back, I can only imagine how hard it must have been for her to tell me the truth—my father left before I was born and they made an agreement that I would always live with my mum and he would not be part of our lives.

'I was too young to understand. Even my friends who didn't live with their dads still saw them, so I begged and begged and begged her to let me meet him. I would not let the subject drop and in the end she agreed to reach out and ask him. I was so excited, utterly convinced he was waiting for the right moment to swing into my life.' She turned her face away and gathered her hair together, twisting it into a knot that held itself together without any means of support.

When she next spoke, all the musicality in her voice had gone. 'She got the reply on a Saturday. I only remem-ber that because I was watching cartoons in my pyjamas. I was young enough to find post being delivered incredibly exciting and so I grabbed the envelope and gave it to her and...' He heard her swallow before she continued in the same monotone. 'When she'd read it, she picked me up and carried me into the living room and sat me on her lap and wrapped her arms tightly around me and told me that she was very sorry but that he'd said no.'

Although Sebastiano knew she'd never met her father and so had known the outcome, he still flinched. 'How old were you?'

'Five.' Her shoulders hunched up and she whispered, 'So I think that's what made me become the chameleon you think I am.'

'You were looking for love?' he asked into the silence.

Her gaze flickered back to him, surprise ringing from it. 'My mother loved me enough for two parents. She practically smothered me in it. It was rejection I became frightened of. My father didn't abandon me like you said, Sebastiano—he abandoned my mum. Me, he rejected. He rejected me before I was born and he rejected me when I was old enough to want to know him, and...' Her shoulders rose. 'It hurt. Really hurt. If I hadn't had my mum constantly telling me that it wasn't my fault, that it was all him, then God knows what I'd have become, but, even with the security of her love, I couldn't shake the fear that there was something inherently wrong with me and so I became adept at being all things to all people and being whatever I thought they wanted me to be, anything to stop them having an excuse to reject me.' A smile suddenly pulled at her cheeks but there was sadness contained in it. 'I grew out of it eventually. Funnily enough, it was my father who inadvertently gave me the tools to become comfortable in my own skin.'

At his questioning gaze, she explained, 'The letter he sent to my mum—I found it tucked in a drawer when I was fifteen. I'd always assumed he'd written it but it actually came from his solicitor, and it was a threat telling my mum that if she contacted him again, he would take legal action against her for harassment. I knew straight away that it was an empty threat but I also knew why it would have terrified her. I was old enough by then to understand.

'My mum's not academically minded—she left school at sixteen because she struggled so much. My father was a lot older than her but she had no idea he was married. She was crazy about him. As soon as he found out she was pregnant, he ran for the hills. He was rich, not by your standards of course, but rich enough to buy her a small home without his wife's knowledge and manipulative enough to get Mum to sign a document stating the house was in lieu of all future child support. He signed full custody of me over to her and she never saw him again. She was nineteen.'

Sebastiano could feel a pulse in his jaw throbbing in time to the beats of blood pounding in his head.

His investigation into Layla's background had brought to light the basics of this but to actually hear it from her and have it explained so starkly...

'She was nineteen, Sebastiano,' she repeated. 'Her parents were deeply religious and they disowned her. She was all alone in the world with a newborn baby. She had a roof over her head but no means to pay the bills for it. She relied on charity to furnish it. My earliest memory is sitting in an office with a picture book while she cleaned around me. She couldn't afford childcare so she took jobs where I could go with her, and she worked so *hard*. She worked her fingers to the bone while that bastard lived the high life with his real family, and once I understood the full picture, and once I'd stalked my father on social media—well, I stalked his wife; he doesn't use it—and saw how he lavished everything on them while letting us suffer, I found my purpose.'

'The law,' he supplied as the pieces of the jigsaw that was Layla slotted together.

She nodded. 'The money you've given the firm will do more good than you could imagine. If even just a couple of those who promised donations at the wedding keep their word, we'll be able to raise much more aware-ness about what we offer to those who actually need us.'

The pulse in his jaw throbbed even stronger. Years of study and training and Layla earned, by choice, the equivalent of a shop worker's salary, and all to help those too poor or too uneducated to navigate the legal system for themselves. To compare it with his own job, where he oversaw thousands of people turning up to work each day for the sole reason of making the rich even richer, made his guts clench in the most uncomfortable way. He couldn't even say he'd followed the path set for him by his parents and the generations of Russos before him out of duty because that would be a lie. He'd embraced his destiny as soon as he'd been old enough to under-stand what it was.

His bank and its divisions around the world played lip service to charity in a variety of ways but it was all corporate dress-up, a means of gaining social kudos and brownie points.

Layla and her firm didn't just talk the talk. They

walked it in the cheapest shoes they could afford so as to leave more money in the coffers for the clients who needed it.

No one could be that selfless. Angels did not exist any more than miracles did.

Angels certainly did not handcuff people to beds and demand five million pounds from them.

'Are you going to use the law to make your father pay?' he asked. That was what he would do if his father had treated him and his mother the way Layla's father had. He would burn for revenge, and as flames licked in his chest, he understood they were flames burning for the need for vengeance for Layla.

For the second time that evening, surprise rang from the forget-me-nots. 'And destroy his children...my half-siblings? No way. They're innocent in all this.'

It wasn't just the pulse in his jaw throbbing now. All his pulses had joined in. 'They're adults.'

'Adults with families of their own who don't deserve to have their lives torn apart.'

'Surely his wife deserves to know?'

'What, like your real wife will know about the mistresses you'll take on the side?'

Breathing heavily through the swathe of rancid emotions churning in him, he stared at her. Sometimes he forgot how much Layla had learned by tending his bar at the club in the years where her every movement around him had been a performance. 'In my world, affairs are conducted discreetly but it is rare that a spouse doesn't know. It is rare for the spouse not to take a lover of their own.'

Colour suffusing her high cheekbones, her musical voice was tight as she said, 'You can fill your boots with mistresses to your heart's content with your future wife but there's no way I'll put up with it.'

His own voice equally tight, he put his arms on the table and leaned his face into hers. 'You agreed to this marriage, Layla. You knew what you were marrying into.'

The flash in her eyes this time was of pure hurt.

Getting to her feet, she said, 'It was marry you or have you destroy the firm that dedicates itself to helping vulnerable people like my mum, so that was hardly a choice, was it? And that's the difference between you and me, Sebastiano—you're happy to destroy innocents whereas I've only ever wanted to help them. I've never wanted to hurt anyone.'

'Where are you going?' he demanded as she headed towards the bifold doors back into the villa.

'To bed. I've developed a headache so feel free to sleep in a guest suite. I'm sure your staff are quite convinced enough already that this marriage is *genuine*.'

CHAPTER ELEVEN

LAYLA HAD LOCKED herself in the bathroom, showered, then thrown on the least sexy knickers she could find and the longest dress before climbing into bed. If the bedroom door had a lock on it, she'd have turned the key.

Unable to sleep…well, it wasn't particularly late, the sun still not having fully set…she scrolled through her phone and tried to convince herself it was the earliness of the evening making her feel all upset and angst-ridden. Tried to convince herself, too, that the reason she kept blinking was because she was tired and not because she was furiously trying to stop tears falling, and she didn't care if she was contradicting herself with her own thoughts.

She'd received a message from the conveyancer acting on her behalf for the purchase of the suburban house, which only added to her upset. Apparently it wasn't possible to fast-track the purchase even though there was no chain, which she knew was utter twaddle. She'd bet the whole five million pounds sitting in her bank account that if Sebastiano had asked the question the purchase would complete so quickly she'd get whiplash.

She'd just fired a message to her mum when she heard movement outside the door and almost gave herself actual whiplash by throwing herself onto her side and shoving her phone under the pillow.

She closed her eyes just as the door handle turned and played at being asleep, hoping, not for the first time, that Sebastiano was deaf to the sound of her thundering heartbeats.

She wished she'd chosen a more comfortable position to feign sleep in.

When the bed dipped, she suddenly found it impossible to feign rhythmic breaths, and when a warm, lean body pressed itself against her, an arm wrapped around her waist and a mouth kissed the top of her head, the tears she'd been fighting for the last hour filled her eyes.

'I'm sorry,' Sebastiano said heavily into her hair.

There was the slightest softening in her rigid form.

He kissed her again and sighed. He still didn't quite understand how they'd gone from bliss to poison in less than an hour but knew he'd been the driving force behind it. And all because the sight of Layla's visibly pregnant stomach had set off emotions in him he didn't know how to decipher and the starkness of her story of abandonment and rejection by her father had turned those emotions into something hot and rancid.

Layla hadn't just been rejected by her father, he thought with an ache in his chest, but her grandparents too. Rejected before she was even born.

Wrapping himself tighter around her, he pressed his palm to the small bump of her belly. 'I swear to you, on my own life, that the life growing beneath my hand will always have a father in me. They will be my heir and I will love them because they are innocent in all this. I will never abandon them and I will never reject them.'

Especially not now that he knew her story and not just the facts set out as a timeline.

It was incomprehensible to him that a man could abandon their own child to poverty. His family weren't perfect—something his mother would probably disagree with—and he knew there were secret children stashed away within the family tree, but those children had not been left to suffer in poverty.

The rush of relief when Layla rolled over to face him was like a tightly coiled spring releasing.

Disconcerted at the strength of it and equally disconcerted at how deeply it cut to see the remnant of the upset he'd caused her reflecting in her eyes, he tried to lighten the tension. 'As for the taking of a mistress… What man would want a mistress if he has a Layla in his bed?'

'What about when I'm the size of a whale?' she whispered.

He rubbed the tip of his nose to hers. 'If you don't want me to take a mistress then I won't.'

Their eyes held.

He had another disconcerting feeling that she was trying to reach into his mind, and then she sighed and lifted a hand to his hair. Softly, she said, 'I entered this marriage with my eyes open and knowing exactly what I was signing up for, but I'm the product of an affair. Someone always gets hurt.'

And Layla could not explain even to herself why it felt like a knife in her heart that Sebastiano would only refrain from taking a mistress while they were married because she didn't want him to. Not because he didn't want to.

Just to imagine him with anyone else brought on instant nausea. To imagine herself with anyone else...

She couldn't. She could not imagine walking away from this marriage and being with anyone else. The thought of touching another man was as repulsive as imagining Sebastiano with another woman, which was exactly why she needed to think of him only as her lover. Because one day he would be someone else's husband. He would belong to someone else.

Layla rarely spoke about her father, had never confided the story about begging her mum to let her meet him to anyone before. Telling Sebastiano the story had been painful, the memories stirring the pain she'd experienced in those long ago days like an echo in her heart.

Fear suddenly raced like cold needles up her spine, and when he said, 'I will never do anything to hurt you, *cara*,' she dug her fingers through his hair to his skull and kissed him as hard as she'd ever kissed him before.

As he snaked his way down her body, kissing and touching her all the way down to her pelvis, she screwed her eyes shut and prayed for the pleasure to drive out the fear that the echoed memories of pain in her heart were nothing but a taster of the pain Sebastiano could inflict on her.

Her last thought before the bliss of his tongue drove her to ecstasy was that she needed to guard her heart much more tightly. Sebastiano was her lover, their marriage a performance. She must remember that. She must.

An overrunning meeting in Frankfurt meant that when Sebastiano arrived back at the villa, he waited in the car for Layla to join him.

The closest he could come to describing the feelings in his stomach on the drive home was butterflies. Whatever the feeling, when she appeared moments after the car came to a stop, the butterflies dived into his chest and extended their wings inside it.

She glided out of the front door and past the statues of scholars bathed in early-autumn sunshine, and as she stepped to the car, the backdrop of the villa and the golden glow suffusing her formed an angelic aura that dazzled him with the same strength as when she'd walked down the aisle to him.

So taken was he by the vision that he didn't notice the phone stuck to her ear until she slid beside him and mouthed, Sorry.

It was not the greeting he'd envisaged after their first night apart since their wedding.

Just one night away from her and her beauty had grown. His expert eye noted her breasts, jutting against her red maxi-dress, had grown too and that the neat little bump that would shortly be scanned at the private hospital used by generations of Russos was more prominent than he remembered.

She ended her call with a long exhale before finally bestowing her attention upon him. 'Sorry about that. Good trip?'

He bit back the churlish answer he wanted to throw at her and leaned in for a kiss that was far too brief for his liking, especially when he'd spent the journey back to her fantasising about the passionate kiss she would greet him with. 'Productive. Who were you talking to? It sounded important.'

'My conveyancer—the solicitor who's supposed to be arranging the purchase of the house for me.'

It took a moment for this to digest. 'You're buying a house?'

'I put the offer in when I first got here. I'd viewed it the weekend before you kidnapped me and it's perfect.'

Her blithe reminder of why she'd married him twisted his guts. 'Perfect for what?'

'A family.'

'And you didn't think to mention this to me?'

Surprise lit her face. 'But I did. I told you I wanted the money to buy a house for me and the baby.'

'You have a home,' he pointed out, finding himself having to swallow back his temper. 'Here with me.'

'But it won't be for ever, and besides I'm desperate to get Mum out of that hellhole.' She gritted her teeth and gave another long exhale. 'She's finally agreed to move into it but the longer it all drags on, the more I worry she'll change her mind. If she refuses to move when the purchase goes through I'll have to get you to kidnap her.'

'Good to know you have uses for me,' he said with only faint sarcasm.

Her eyebrow rose. 'What does that mean?'

He had to take a long breath of his own before he trusted himself to answer.

It was sheer arrogance that had let him assume Layla would have missed him during their first night apart in three weeks. It hadn't occurred to him that he would miss her, not until he'd found himself in his apartment contemplating flying home for a few hours and then returning to Frankfurt first thing.

From the way Layla was acting, he might as well have been gone only ten minutes.

Keeping his tone moderate, he said, 'Layla, I have just learned you are buying a home without my knowledge and that you're trying to move your mother out of the house you've just described as a hellhole. Do you not think these are things you should have discussed with me?'

She looked nonplussed.

'I'm your husband.' Did she just *flinch* at that? 'You should discuss important things with me.'

'Do you discuss important things with me?'

'If I had important things to discuss then I would.' He took another deep breath. He didn't want an argument. That night on their honeymoon when bliss had turned to poison still lingered in him, although he had no clue why. Neither of them had mentioned it again. They'd returned home and embarked on married life, and for all that it was proving to be working well between them—better than even he'd hoped—and for all the copious amounts of sex they enjoyed together, he couldn't shake the feeling that they were building a marriage on sand. 'Tell me about this house.'

Her gaze troubled, she sighed. 'The prospectus is still online.'

After she'd recited the address, he found it.

'It's small,' he observed.

'It's huge compared to my old house.'

He scrolled for more information on it. 'It's in a good neighbourhood,' he eventually said, 'but installing adequate security will be impossible.'

'I don't need security.'

He raised an eyebrow. 'You're my wife. Your child will be a Russo. They will be a target for kidnappers. I'm sorry, Layla, but this is completely unsuitable.' He then proceeded to tell her exactly why it was unsuitable, making such a good fist of it that she'd turned quite pale by the time he'd finished.

'I have a proposition,' he told her as they turned onto the long drive that led to the hospital. 'We can look for a suitable house together which I will buy but have put in your name. We can use it as our London base.'

As of next Monday, Layla would spend her working weeks in London as had been pre-agreed. They'd only spoken about it in vague terms but it was something that had played on his mind since the honeymoon. Sebastiano's rarely used apartment in central London would work fine for a baby but not an inquisitive toddler. They needed a proper home there, and Layla had given him the perfect opening to suggest it.

'We?' she queried.

'I will arrange my schedule so I can be London-based as much as is practicable. We are newly-weds,' he reminded her. 'This is our honeymoon stage. If we spend too much time apart too soon then people will talk.'

Layla's top teeth grazed harder than normal into her bottom lip as she held herself back from reminding him that she was buying the house for her and their baby for when their marriage was over. She'd already envisaged how she would furnish it, the colour schemes, the bedroom she'd create for the little life steadily growing inside her. And as for London...

She'd assumed Sebastiano would resume his normal working life and the copious amount of travelling it involved once their honeymoon was over. So far, though, he'd taken to working from his home office with alarming frequency, only the most important meetings taking him out of their Sicilian home.

She hadn't factored in how determined he was to promote a *genuine* marriage to the world, and as a result she'd had little respite from him. She'd sit in her office and liaise with clients and colleagues and create documents and fill out paperwork entirely aware that Sebastiano was working on the other side of the door. Entirely aware. They shared all their meals together and then at night, they closed the bedroom door and fell into each other's arms.

How was she supposed to remember that this was all a performance when they were so rarely apart and when Sebastiano was treating her as if she were his real wife? It was becoming impossible.

What made it worse were the times they did spend apart. The times when she sat in her office wholly aware of his absence. And then last night she'd slept alone and it had been awful. For the first time since arriving in Sicily, her insomnia had kicked back in. She'd been unable to settle the whole night through, sleep coming only in brief snatches.

She needed some proper separation. She'd been banking on having Mondays to Fridays away from him, a chance to create physical and emotional distance. Because that was the worst thing of all. How emotionally attached she was becoming to him. The reason she daydreamed about the home that would be hers when their marriage ended was because she knew she had to.

But she was being backed into a corner. It was too

soon after their wedding to start sowing the seeds of distance that would be used to explain their marriage failing. It was unthinkable that Sebastiano would let it end before the baby was born. Speculation was already rife in the press that she was pregnant, her small bump captured in a photo during an evening gala going a long way in proving their marriage was genuine.

What frightened her more than anything was what came after the baby was born and the DNA test proved beyond doubt that it was his. What if he decided this meant their marriage should continue indefinitely, something she suspected he was already thinking? What if he didn't? She didn't know which scenario frightened her the most. If he wanted them to stay together it would only be because of their child. If he let her go it would be to produce a spare to her baby's heir with another woman. Either way, Layla lost. Either way, she wouldn't be enough for him as she was, and though she knew she shouldn't care if she was enough for him, it was becoming increasingly hard to deny that she did care. Cared more than was healthy or safe.

'You don't look happy at the prospect,' he observed, cutting through her unhappy musings, his eyes narrowed with shrewdness.

For a moment, she feared she would cry.

She couldn't tell him why she looked unhappy. She knew she should be grateful that he was taking their baby's security so seriously even while doubting it was his, be grateful too at his vow that he would be a father to it whatever a DNA test might say, and grateful that he was taking the pregnancy and birth seriously enough that he wanted her to be cared for in Sicily's most eminent private hospital.

And so she swallowed back her dejection.

'I can see that it makes sense,' she said. And she *could* see it, much as she wished she couldn't, and much as she wished she could think of the perfect counterargument. 'But what about my mum?'

'She can move into the London place with us. She can live here with us too.'

Her mouth dropped open in astonishment.

He raised a nonchalant shoulder. 'We will make sure the London property has a self-contained flat or a separate dwelling on the grounds for her. Here, she can take her pick of the guest cottages.'

'Are you serious?'

Please, Sebastiano, say no. Don't do something else wonderful for me. I need to hate you more than love... like you.

He fixed her with a stare that read, 'do you have to ask?'

She had to turn her face away briefly to blink back tears without him seeing. 'You'd be happy for my *mum* to live with us?'

He tutted and folded his arms across his chest. 'I'm Sicilian. Family is everything to us, and your mother is everything to you.'

The tears pooled back, hot and brimming, and she turned away again, pretending to be transfixed with the sprawling white building their driver had come to a stop at.

In England, she'd already be out of the car and hurrying inside, afraid of being late for her appointment.

Here, in this exclusive private hospital with its manicured grounds that only the ridiculously rich could afford, they would wait for her. After all, she was no longer plain Layla Sansom. She was the great Sebastiano Russo's wife.

'She won't agree,' she eventually said when she was semi-certain she could speak without choking.

'Why not?'

'I only managed to convince her to move to the suburban house by selling the garden to her—gardening's her therapy. She sits in our little garden with a cup of tea and manages to forget that the house next door is a narcotic shop and that the vampires all descend on the street at night.' She closed her eyes and laughed sadly. 'She has this amazing ability to tune out the terrible stuff and laser in on the good stuff. She turned that house into a home for us. She painted every wall and hung every curtain and it became her sanctuary from the world when she was at her most scared and vulnerable. She's frightened of leaving it. No way will she agree to move countries.'

Sebastiano digested this, breathing hard to smother the anger that had flared, not with Layla but with himself. He knew how desperate Layla had been to move out of that house before their baby was born and should have realised she'd want her mother moved out of it too. Jilly Sansom was his mother-in-law and so a part of his extended family. Her safety was as much his responsibility as her daughter and grandchild's safety.

He gave a sharp nod. 'Will you let me talk to her?'

Her gaze moved from the window to him. 'And say what?'

He tapped her nose and forced a smile. 'Trust me to find the right words.'

She responded with a smile of her own that looked as forced as his felt. 'I know I said about you kidnapping her, but no handcuffs, okay?'

This time he smiled with his whole face, capturing her cheeks in his hand and releasing some of the angst knotted in his chest in a deep, passionate kiss. 'Believe me, my little rabbit,' he murmured, 'you are the only person I wish to use handcuffs on.'

Layla felt like she'd entered a five-star hotel rather than a hospital. The only difference was the faint trace of disinfectant that permeated the walls.

A manager escorted them down a wide, thickly carpeted corridor to the maternity wing, explaining in perfect English all the facilities they had to offer the expectant mother and the excellent care she could expect. After a full tour of the birthing wing, Layla's mind was made up. This was the hospital she would have her baby in.

By the time they entered the clinical room for her scan and she lay on the bed and lifted her top to expose her naked bump, she was filled to the brim with excitement. The first scan had been the most magical moment of her life and she'd counted down the days until she could see her baby again...

She caught the look on Sebastiano's face and her heart sank.

There was no mirroring of her excitement there.

After a beat, she turned her stare from him, smiled at the sweet-faced sonographer, and fixed her gaze on the computer screen beside her.

She would not let his lack of visible excitement ruin this moment for her.

* * *

The rapid thuds of the baby's heartbeat were much louder than Sebastiano had anticipated. They filled the room.

The beats of his own heart accelerated.

A mass appeared on the computer screen. The sonographer pressed the ultrasound probe down on the left of Layla's belly. The screen became clearer. Suddenly he could discern a head...a belly...limbs...

White noise filled his head. He could no longer distinguish the individual beats battering against his ribs.

'Is the baby the right size?' he heard Layla ask, her anxious voice distant, as if she were far away rather than right beside him.

'Let me take the measurements to be sure,' the sonographer answered. 'You are worried?'

'A little,' she confessed. 'It's only because my bump's so small.'

She was worried about that?

Still pressing the probe to Layla's stomach, the sonographer tapped at her computer's keyboard with her other hand.

Sebastiano hadn't realised he'd been holding his breath until the sonographer smiled and it escaped in a rush.

'All normal,' she said. 'Your baby's rate of growth is perfect. Everything is normal and how it should be.'

There was no mistaking the relief on Layla's face.

No mistaking, either, the relief washing through *him*.

'Would you like to know the sex?'

For the first time since she'd climbed on the medical bed, Layla turned her stare from the screen and looked at him. There was a question in her eyes. And a plea that made his still rapidly beating heart catch and his head pound.

She was pleading with him to believe her...

He cleared his throat but couldn't clear the pounding. 'Do you want to know?'

She shook her head.

'Then let it be a surprise.'

In the car on their return to the villa, Sebastiano's heart had finally decreased back to a relatively normal beat but the throbbing in his head remained. Watching Layla stare reverently at the scan photo of the baby deepened the throbs.

Keeping his voice measured, he casually said, 'I didn't know you were worried about the baby's size.'

She pressed the photo to her chest, right over her heart, then slipped it into her handbag. 'It was more a minor concern than a worry. You know, one of those things that sit in the back of your mind and niggle at you?'

He did know. Layla's behaviour was his own *niggle*. 'Why didn't you tell me?'

Her forehead furrowed. 'I never thought to. It was only a niggle.'

He held onto his temper by the skin of his teeth. That was twice in three hours he'd learned something important Layla had kept from him.

'*Cara,*' he said, taking her hand, 'you cannot keep hiding things from me. If you have worries you must share them with me.'

Although Layla knew she shouldn't feel guilty, it still stabbed at her. But if he wanted honesty from her...

'It wasn't intentional,' she said quietly. 'I think it's

knowing you don't believe the baby is yours… It's making it difficult for me to open up about the pregnancy to you.' Increasingly difficult. He was doing everything an expectant father should but it all felt clinical, like he was going through the motions without his heart being in it.

She'd seen his reflection on the computer screen. While she'd been thrilling to see their baby, Sebastiano's face had been emotionless. And all because he couldn't admit to himself that the baby was his.

'Listen to me,' he said firmly. 'What I believe is irrelevant. The baby is mine. I will always be its father and I will always be there for you. Trust that, Layla, and stop shutting me out. We are in this together.'

Oh, how she *longed* to believe him.

Longed with all her heart.

CHAPTER TWELVE

SINCE LAYLA HAD cuffed Sebastiano to a bed, she'd suffered a cricked neck and virtual whiplash. Now she was close to getting real whiplash such was the speed Sebastiano had moved. One day he'd asked her to trust him to find the right words to convince her mother to move, the next he'd flown to London, returning in time for dinner with a smile of satisfaction.

Whatever he'd said to her mother to convince her to move in with them was being kept secret by them both, but convince her he had. The very next day her mother had arrived in Sicily and chosen a guest house to make herself a home in.

So much had her mother fallen in love with Sicily and the 'cosy' garden that came with it, which was three times the size of their London garden, that within weeks of moving in she was happier than Layla could ever remember. Such happiness did she radiate that Layla had felt compelled to gently remind her that it wouldn't be for ever. Her marriage came with its end already written.

'It will all work out for the best,' her mum had said with a smile. 'You'll see.'

But best for whom? That was all Layla could wonder. And because it made her heart hurt to wonder too much, she threw herself into her work, using her free time to chase up the wedding guests who'd indicated they would like to make donations to the firm.

The money came through thick and fast and accumulated so quickly that when Sebastiano suggested over a dinner with Laurence and his husband that they should think about increasing their team's salaries to make themselves more competitive to new recruits, they hadn't dismissed it with a laugh. They had laughed though, in sheer joyful disbelief, when he offered them the use of a floor of Russo Banca Internazionale's London skyscraper in the financial district. Layla had laughed too because if she'd gone with the alternative, crying, she might be crying still.

It was the most wonderful gesture from Sebastiano. The floor he gave them was three times the size of the floor they'd occupied for three decades and he was giving it rent free for a guaranteed minimum of twenty years. A week after moving into it, Clayton Community Law had a list of potential recruits wanting to join the firm when they graduated. Enquiries for placements were coming as thick and fast as the money, and now they had the difficult task of sifting the recruits for those genuinely wanting to join a philanthropic law firm rather than those wanting a fat salary and an office with a view. It was a nice but ultimately serious problem to have because the only thing they couldn't afford was to recruit someone unable to treat their clients with respect.

Layla had problems of her own with the move and all the changes, and they were entirely selfish. The move meant she had no respite from Sebastiano at all. Even when he was away travelling, she now worked from a building he owned. She walked into the lobby and was greeted by his enlarged photo flanked by photos of the heads of divisions and countries. She stepped into the elevator and knew it was an elevator he'd taken. She dined in the staff canteen that was as much a canteen as an orange was a pear. The food served was exquisite, table service given, a wine menu…she'd dined in worse award-winning restaurants and it was all because Sebastiano insisted on it. And insisted on heavily subsidising it.

She couldn't even settle at her desk without thinking of him because the very chair she sat on had been imported from Japan especially for her, a fancy ergonomic chair designed for pregnant women.

Within three months of their marriage, Sebastiano had infected her entire life and everyone in it, and all she could do was follow the lead of the character of her favourite childhood film and just keep swimming. The alternative, she very much feared, was to drown.

Layla stood in her Sicilian dressing room trying to decide which of the fresh batch of evening dresses made for her that she should wear to the evening's party. She'd needed to expand her wardrobe to accommodate her expanding belly. Now she was seven months pregnant, her bump was still small but it had grown enough that her clothes had laughed at her when she tried to make them fit.

Just as she'd settled on a floaty red dress, something caught her eye out of the window. Her heart was thrashing even before she recognised the car heading down the long driveway.

Sebastiano was home.

Five nights without him. The longest they'd ever been parted.

Enduring it had been hell.

Gripping tightly to the window sill, she fought the compulsion to go skipping down the stairs to greet him. She needed to compose herself first, couldn't bear to think of him looking into her eyes and seeing how desperately she'd missed him.

By arranging herself with a book on the chaise longue that ran beneath one of the sash windows, she hoped Sebastiano would find in her a woman enjoying a lazy Saturday afternoon. She hoped, too, that he wouldn't look too closely at her face or he'd notice the puffiness of her eyes that five nights of insomnia had caused and which gel eye patches followed by expensive concealer had barely reduced.

Sebastiano bounded up the stairs stifling the disappointment at the lack of soft lips and warm body waiting impatiently at the front door to greet his return. The butler had informed him that Layla was resting.

She was seven months pregnant, he reminded himself. Her bump might be smaller than in the average pregnancy but the effects on her body were the same. The emotional effects were the same.

It was something he had to continually remind himself of because on the surface, Sebastiano had a marriage most of the men he knew could only dream about.

Layla didn't complain about the hours he worked. She didn't complain if he had to change plans at the last minute due to issues beyond his control. She didn't ask to accompany him on overnight trips. She didn't demand a blow-by-blow account of how he spent his time when he was away from her.

He would prefer it if she did. At least it would show she cared.

His footsteps slowed as he trod the mezzanine to their room, a tightness forming in the chest that had been pounding in anticipation of seeing her again.

For the woman who'd flushed with anger at the thought of him taking a mistress, he'd now be surprised if she'd give a damn if he did it.

The temptation was there, to take himself a lover just to see how she'd react. There were two things stopping him. One was the promise he'd made. The other was that he had no interest in anyone else. Even when alone in bed, his fantasies revolved only around Layla.

It had reached the stage where his whole world revolved around her.

Her world did not revolve around him.

On the surface, she performed as perfectly as she ever had. She was still the perfect public wife, the perfect hostess, the perfect daughter-in-law and member of the Russo empire. She was always—always—the perfect bed partner, as unable to keep her hands off him as he was unable to keep his hands off her.

She was perfect in every way and yet...

And yet when they were apart he doubted she spared him a thought. All messages and calls these last five days had been instigated by him.

He could forgive her disinterest if he thought it was the pregnancy and her job consuming her to the point of her blocking everything else out, but Layla's disinterest ran deeper than that. She'd closed a part of herself off from him and the longer their marriage went on, the more intensely he felt it and the more it ate at him.

He opened the bedroom door.

She was reclining on a chaise longue beneath a window, reading.

The light that ignited in her eyes to see him eased a little of the tightness.

'You're back,' she sang, discarding the book without saving the page and easing herself up. Padding over to him with a grace that not even seven months of pregnancy could diminish, she threw her arms around his neck.

The welcome heat of her passionate kiss overrode the rest of the tightness, and he returned it with all the hunger that had built during those interminably long days apart.

Only when the hunger had been temporarily sated enough did he break away to cup her cheeks and gaze at the face he'd missed so much that at times it had been hard to breathe.

Her cheeks were flushed, the forget-me-nots pulsing their desire.

Whatever else his wife might feel, this was the one area where the closeness between them could not be broken, and he brought his face back to hers. *'Mi sei mancata tantissimo,'* he murmured before smothering her with another deeply passionate kiss.

Layla's intention to play it cool had been forgotten the moment Sebastiano walked through the door. The joy that had careered through her had been too powerful to resist.

When, she wondered dimly as she revelled at being

back in his arms and having his taste fill her senses, would she reach the point when she could look at Sebastiano and be able to breathe normally? When longing wouldn't grip her so tightly? When she wouldn't experience such a dizzying rush just to breathe his cologne?

In moments she was carefully lifted into the air and sat on the edge of the bed.

Between biting kisses, they stripped his polo shirt and her cashmere sweater, her bra swiftly following. And then he gently pushed her on her back to assault her senses, trailing hot kisses down her throat and to her breasts, kissing, licking and nipping while he slipped a hand up her short skirt and cupped her heat. Knickers yanked down her thighs and calves, she kicked them off and spread her thighs as she reached for his chinos. Expertly, she undid the button and lowered the zip, then tugged his chinos and underwear down to his thighs and took him, huge and fully erect in her hand. While his fingers pleasured her between her legs and his mouth and tongue worked their magic on her breasts, she masturbated him, bringing him closer to her heat so that when he moved his hand away from her heat, he could drive straight inside her.

She moaned loudly as he filled her and wrapped her legs tight around his waist.

This was what she missed when he was away from her, she tried desperately to tell herself. His lovemaking. The feeling of complete and utter sensory overload that she could only get from Sebastiano.

Lying back, she closed her eyes and revelled in every thrust and every burning sensation.

His fingers found hers and threaded through them.

She squeezed back.

The tempo increased. The sensory pleasure was almost more than she could endure, burning through every cell, the swell of her orgasm building and building until it exploded in a tidal wave of sensation that had her open her eyes as she cried out and lifted her head for his kiss.

Eyes dark and hooded, he kissed her hard through the grunts of his own pleasure and then, with one long final thrust, he climaxed. The pressure of his groin against hers in that final thrust set off one final wave of bliss through her and as she rode it, their mouths fused, Sebastiano so deep inside her he could be a part of her, a wave of something else, something new, broke free and rippled through her with the strength to make her cry out again, louder than she had ever done.

The wave came from her heart.

It took a long time for the thrills of his orgasm to subside. Even longer for Sebastiano to bring himself to break away from Layla and roll onto his side.

The beats of his heart echoing and pulsing through his skin, he inhaled deeply in an effort to bring himself fully back to earth.

After all this time, how could it just keep getting better and better between them?

Fingers laced with hers, he stared intently into her eyes and wished he could read what she was thinking as she gazed with equal intensity back at him.

There was a wanness to her features that he hadn't noticed earlier. Faint shadows beneath her eyes.

Had he got it all wrong about her feelings for him? Could it be that she simply respected that when he was away on business, he was working and so didn't want to bother him with frivolous calls or messages?

Was it possible that Layla really *had* missed him?

Was it possible, Layla wondered helplessly as she gazed into Sebastiano's green depths, that he'd missed her even a little bit? Missed *her*, not just the mind-blowing sex they shared?

'We should think about getting ready for the party,' he murmured. 'Especially if you want to have a bath before we leave.'

'Probably,' she whispered. She was in no rush to leave this bed.

No rush to *ever* leave this bed. To ever leave him...

A wave of emotion rushed through her, strong enough to fill her eyes with tears.

Concern filled *his* eyes. *'Cara?'*

With a sniff, she blinked the tears away and smiled. 'Our baby's kicking.'

'And that makes you cry?'

No, it's the thought of having to lose you that hurts my heart so much it makes me want to weep. 'I'm just feeling a bit emotional.'

'Can I feel?'

Her heart hitched. Sebastiano never asked to feel their baby. 'Do you want to?'

'Very much.' The sincerity in his voice and stare made her heart hitch again.

Covering his hand, she placed it on the part of her belly the kicks were coming.

Sebastiano's hand rested on her bump so long without anything happening that he thought the baby had gone back to sleep.

And then he felt it. An indentation against his palm.

Awed, he laughed at the sheer strangeness of it.

'It's something, isn't it?' she said softly, eyes now shining with something very different from the tears that had filled them only minutes ago.

There was another kick against his palm.

The ripples kicked straight into his heart then pulsed through every inch of his being.

That was his baby.

His and Layla's baby.

The bedroom was empty once Sebastiano had showered, shaved and donned the shirt and trousers of his tuxedo. He caught the scent of steamy cherry blossom and guessed Layla was in the bath.

Knocking on the door first, he poked his head around it and, despite all the emotions still careering through him, grinned to find her submerged in thick, foamy bubbles, her hair piled on top of her head, reading. 'You'll get the pages wet.'

She grinned back. 'Then invent waterproof books for me.'

'Beyond my skillset. I'm going to fix myself a drink.' As much as he would like to carry her out of the bath, lay her back on the bed and devour her all over again, Layla's daily bath was her way of dealing with the pregnancy backache she'd recently started experiencing. 'Can I get you anything?'

'I'm good, thanks.'

'Don't be too long,' he warned gently. 'The helicopter will be here in an hour.'

'I'll finish this chapter and then get out. It won't take me long to get ready.'

Blowing her a kiss, he went downstairs, poured himself a much-needed large Scotch and then headed to his office to check his upcoming schedule.

So many thoughts were crowding him, jostling with all the emotions fighting for space. He, the man who *never* allowed emotions to dictate his actions, had found himself close to being paralysed with them.

He needed to focus on something tangible, hence his decision to go through his schedule. Because he couldn't go on like this. He needed to do something about all the travelling that was keeping him apart from Layla, find a way to condense it even more than his assistant had already managed for him.

At one point he'd had the wild idea of suggesting she work remotely from Sicily for a few days each week. His headquarters were in Sicily. It meant they would be able to spend more time together. He'd rejected the idea because he'd known *she* would reject it.

It was a thought that lowered his buoyant mood a couple of degrees.

Not wanting a repeat of the poison that had started to fill his veins earlier on his walk to their bedroom, he took a drink of his Scotch and firmly reminded himself that he had a great marriage.

Wondering what Layla's schedule was like for the next few weeks, he crossed the dividing door to her now rarely used office. Giovanna, like Sebastiano's own assistant, faithfully reproduced Layla's schedule in an office planner kept on Layla's desk.

Post had been neatly piled on the desk. From the size

of it, she hadn't been in here since her return from London the day before.

The franking mark on the top envelope caught his eye.

He picked it up to look more closely. Why would Layla be getting post from a London-based conveyancing firm? Any work-related post was sent to her offices in London...

His fingers had ripped the envelope open before he could stop them.

Layla checked her appearance one last time. She really loved this red dress. It was simply cut with her favoured spaghetti straps and just the right side of elegant without constricting her waist. On her feet she wore funky black shoes with a small heel. She was too pregnant for stilettos now, but not too pregnant for her favourite pair of giant hooped gold earrings. Her hair she'd left loose, her makeup a touch of black mascara and a dash of red lipstick to match her dress.

With a spritz of her favourite—and Sebastiano's favourite—perfume, she left the bedroom and set off to find him.

Strangely, she couldn't find him in any of the usual rooms. A further search proved *all* the rooms of the villa were empty of him. None of the staff had seen him.

Trying to quell her unease, she called his mobile. No answer.

A check of the security cameras showed he hadn't left the villa.

After three calls, four text messages, numerous shouts of his name and fifteen minutes of searching, she heard the sound of rotors. Their helicopter was landing. So where was Sebastiano?

About to go back upstairs and check the bedrooms again, she stopped. There was one room she hadn't looked in.

Her back now aching after all this searching, she set off again to his office. The door that adjoined her office, the one room she hadn't checked, was closed.

She opened it and her heart froze.

Sebastiano sat behind her desk, an empty crystal glass in front of him. All her drawers were open. Papers were heaped all over the desk and all over the floor.

He smiled. If a heart could freeze twice, that smile did it. 'Hello, Layla. Good of you to join me.'

The chill in her chest spreading through her veins at a rate of knots, Layla folded her arms over her stomach and absently rubbed the spot she could feel her baby's back nestled against it as it slept. 'What are you doing?'

'Me?' His smile widened and suddenly she was thrown back to the day he'd blackmailed her into their marriage.

This was the smile of the big cat before it ate its prey...

'I'm not doing anything.' If she closed her eyes she could hear the purred undertone. 'Unless you consider me going through all the paperwork in my wife's office as doing something?'

A drum was beating in her ear. She was almost too afraid to blink.

'Tell me, *wife*, when were you planning to tell me that you bought the house? You know the house I mean? The one that you agreed was an unsuitable home to raise our child in? The one you have already installed a panic room in.'

The blood in her head drained to her feet so quickly that she sagged back against the door. If it hadn't been there she would have fallen.

Eyes not leaving her face, he leaned forwards. The big cat showed its teeth. 'The house, Layla.'

CHAPTER THIRTEEN

SEBASTIANO WATCHED THE host of emotions flitter over Layla's beautiful face and, without any warning, the anger he'd been containing by the skin of his teeth erupted. 'Tell me!' he shouted, getting to his feet and slamming his palm on the desk. 'Tell me why you have gone behind my back after everything we discussed, everything we agreed, you conniving—' He bit back the curse he wanted to hurl at her and took a large lungful of air.

His instincts had been right all along.

Layla had been keeping a part of herself separate from him. A major part.

His perfect wife had gone against his wishes and behind his back to provide herself with the perfect bolt-hole to raise his child without him,

'I have given you *everything* in this marriage, Layla. Everything. And this is how you repay me. With deceit.'

'Deceit?' Eyes wide, she shook her head tremulously. 'I didn't go ahead with the house purchase because I was being deceitful or conniving—I bought it because I've spent our entire marriage terrified of the day you wake up and decide I've served my purpose, and get your big fancy lawyers on me and leave me with nothing.' Her voice caught. 'I'm sorry if you feel betrayed but that money was all I had that you couldn't touch. I needed to put it in a home that would provide safety for me and my baby if the day ever came that we needed it.'

'Safety from me?' he roared, incredulous. 'After everything I've done for you?'

'Done for your own conscience you mean,' she countered before closing her eyes. Taking a deep breath, she fixed her stare back on him and gave a helpless shrug. 'I never asked for *any* of this. All I ever wanted from you was support for my baby.'

'*Our* baby,' he corrected, unmoved.

The expression on her face at this would have made the stoniest heart laugh, but all he could manage was one laced with bitterness. 'Yes, Layla. I know the child is mine.' The truth had been knocking at him for so long…right from the start…that he couldn't pinpoint when he'd accepted it in his heart, but the emotions that had swelled in him to feel it kick against his hand earlier had blown the last of the denial out of him. 'I feel it here.' He slammed his palm onto his heart. 'Right in the place I used to feel you. And now I'm done. I'm done with trying to make you happy and fulfilled when you couldn't give a damn about me.'

Done with a marriage that had never gone beyond a performance and a wife who made promises she had no intention of keeping.

'That's not true!' she cried. 'Of course I–'

'No more lies,' he snarled before clenching his jaw and dragging air into his lungs in an effort to temper his tone. Never in the whole of his life had he felt infected by such hot, rancid emotions. 'I'm leaving. You have the night to get your stuff together—the staff will help you. I'll be back by breakfast. Make sure you're gone before I return.'

Her mouth dropped open in shock. It took an age for anything to come out of it. 'You're ending our marriage, *now*?' she croaked.

He looked her dead in the eye.

Dio, he was having to stop himself from shaking.

'Oh, no,' he said tightly. 'Having given it some serious thought I've decided we will never divorce. I'm going to hold you to this godforsaken marriage for the rest of your miserable life. It is just that I would rather spend the night in a nest of vipers than spend another night under the same roof as you.'

Layla was trembling so hard she had to cling to the door to keep herself upright. She could hardly believe what was happening, that the man who'd made such passionate love to her such a short time ago could be looking at her with such loathing and uttering words that landed like a wound.

'I will be in touch with instructions on how we will play things from now on, and you will obey them.' He gave a smile so cold and cruel it landed like its own wound. 'Or live with the consequences... Full custody of my child.'

Her heart pounding, she stared at this stranger who'd taken possession of her lover. Of all the ways she'd imagined their marriage ending—imaginings she'd forced on herself because she'd never dared hope this day wouldn't come—she'd never dreamed it would end like this.

'Don't threaten me with our baby, Sebastiano,' she begged. 'Please, don't be that man.'

Something…a glimmer of conscience?…flashed in his eyes.

The cruel smile vanished. His voice stark, he quietly said, 'At least I never set out to make a home for it without you.'

Of all his accusations, that one landed the hardest. She threw her hands in the air, despair ripping through her. 'That's right, assume the worst of me like you always do. The house was only ever a back-up plan for my own peace of mind, and only because I couldn't shake the fear that I'd be left alone to raise our child just like my mother was left alone to raise me.'

She snatched a moment to gather herself against the emotions battering her. 'I always knew you believed the truth about our baby but you couldn't bring yourself to admit it, could you? Because to admit it meant you'd have to accept that you'd failed, and you really can't bear to fail.'

'Do not try and deflect things back on me,' he said through gritted teeth. 'This is all you, Layla.'

'Is it really?' She shook her head. It felt like she'd sleepwalked into a nightmare she couldn't wake herself from. 'I *know* I'm scarred. Living with you has shown me just how scarred I still am, but the difference is I acknowledge it, whereas you… Life has been so gilded and effortless for you, success upon success upon success, that at the first hint of failure you take a child's default position of denial. You denied paternity when I gave you all the proof, and continued denying it. You preferred to believe I must have taken another lover straight after you than admit that at some point during our night together you screwed up. As if the great Sebastiano Russo could have got a lowly bar tender pregnant! What would polite society say about that?'

He made to speak but she wouldn't let him. She couldn't bear to hear another cruel word from his lips.

'If you hadn't discovered that I'm actually a respectable solicitor, you would never have decided to use me in your game of cover up, although what you would have done to gain vengeance against me I can only guess, and what you'd have done to cover up the money loss, again I can only guess. But you'd have thought of something because there is no way the great Sebastiano Russo would hold his hands up and admit that he'd made such a colossal mistake with those shares, or accept that his actions had backed me into such a corner that I acted in a way I should never have acted.'

She could do nothing to stop the tear that rolled down her cheek or stop her voice from breaking. 'You broke my heart, did you know that? You cut me off and acted as if that night meant nothing when you know damned well it meant *everything*.' Her voice broke again but she forced herself to continue. 'I know you'll deny it but something magical happened between us the night we made our child, but you chose to ignore it because you believed I wasn't good enough for you. I'm glad you didn't know I was a solicitor because you probably *would* have deemed me fit to pursue a relationship with and I'd have believed it was because of what you felt for me and not because I ticked the correct boxes for polite society.' She closed her eyes and clung tightly to the door. 'And then you really would have destroyed me.'

The silence that followed this was total.

Opening her eyes, Layla took in Sebastiano's ashen face. Something deep in her heart cracked.

'Do you have any idea how terrified I was when I found out I was pregnant?' she whispered. 'How alone I felt? How desperately hard I tried to reach you? And you have the nerve to act as if you're the injured party and the nerve to expect me to be *grateful*?'

Shaking her head, she took one more deep breath then looked at him for the last time. 'This is your home not mine. You stay. I'll sleep in a guest house tonight and be gone by the morning.'

Layla walked on autopilot through the sprawling rear garden breathing in the wintry air that was nothing like the wintry air she would be breathing in London come the morning. By the marble statue of the Venus de Milo, she took the path that led to the most secluded of the guest cottages. Pretty nightlights led the way.

At the door, she closed her eyes before knocking on it. It opened.

Her mother gazed at her before sympathy creased her face and she held out a hand.

Only when the door closed her in did Layla collapse with loud sobs into her mother's arms.

'Pack it all up and courier it to London. All of it.'

Those were Sebastiano's only instructions, his only hint to the staff that Layla would not be returning.

He supposed he should be thinking about loose lips but he was too numb to care. Let them talk if they wanted.

If they were talking it was not within his earshot. The villa had become as silent as a tomb.

It had become as cold as a tomb too.

On his bureau, the handwritten invitation to a Viennese Ball for the end of March. The baby would be born by then so he'd accepted it weeks ago with stray fantasies of Layla in a ball dress, waltzing in his arms. Stray fantasies, too, of making a long weekend of it, the two of them and their baby. Salzburg was a beautiful city, one he was quite certain Layla would fall in love with.

He ripped the invitation into shreds.

Sebastiano's slightly smiling photo loomed large in the Russo Banca Internazionale foyer.

Layla hunched her shoulders and blocked it out as she had every morning that week.

At her desk, she called the clerk of the court about a case that was being heard on Tuesday. Naturally, her call was held in a queue. It felt like the majority of her time this past week had been spent on hold, and she closed her eyes and suppressed the scream that longed to come out.

It was a scream she'd been suppressing the whole week. The only thing that stopped her releasing it was the baby currently kicking at her ribs. Stress wasn't good for babies so she was doing her best to portray serenity inside and out. Her best, she was painfully aware, wasn't good enough, an awareness reinforced when a box of tissues slid beneath her.

Amelia, who'd entered her office without Layla noticing her, caught her eye and gave a rueful smile.

Smiling gratefully in return, Layla dabbed at eyes she hadn't even realised were leaking and blew her nose. She'd been suffering the most dreadful winter hay fever this past week. The main symptom was leaking eyes. They were like taps she had no control over.

Or so she'd told all her colleagues.

No one knew her marriage was over. Not that her marriage was over in name, just in actuality. She supposed the correct term to describe them was as estranged.

If Sebastiano was true to his word then she would be his legal wife for ever, consigned to live in the purgatory of his whims, brought out like an expensive doll to be draped on his arm whenever duty demanded and then be packed back in a box.

None of that would happen. She knew it in her heart.

For all his threats and the way things had been left between them, she doubted she would see him again until the baby was born. It was the only good thing about the whole sorry mess. Her child really would have a father. And she had a few months to prepare herself emotionally for facing him again.

She was on her third tissue when her call was finally answered.

Late evening, Sebastiano strode to the dressing room that had belonged to Layla. After a day spent avoiding his family's efforts to visit him and speak to him—whispers must be spreading that his marriage was over—he'd decided to do something constructive and so had decided to turn the dressing room into a room his tailor could use for fittings when he made his three-monthly visit to the villa to measure Sebastiano up for new suits. He would not think that if he were measured today, the tailor would find he'd lost weight.

There was no point in letting the room stand empty

with no purpose. It had always been intended as a room for whoever he married. Maybe one day he would marry again and his future wife could have it but until then...

An unexpected blow to his solar plexus almost doubled him over.

It took a long moment to breathe through the pain and straighten.

Where the hell had that come from?

Expelling another breath through his mouth, he turned the door handle. Already his mind was racing ahead, to bringing the master carpenter here to redesign the room. Fresh paint would be needed on the walls too. A new colour scheme. He'd also have to get the 'her' bathroom of his suite redecorated. He'd told the interior designer to go with a Japanese theme because he'd remembered Layla once saying she loved the scent of cherry blossom.

He'd never told Layla the bathroom had been created especially for her and only finished the evening before he'd brought her to Sicily.

Kidnapped her, a voice in his head corrected.

He opened the door and stepped inside.

The emptiness hit him immediately.

He'd expected it. He'd ordered it be stripped bare.

Seeing it though... Feeling it...

This went beyond emptiness. This was absence.

A scent danced through his senses and into his airwaves and for a moment, just one solitary moment in time, he saw her. Layla. Hair tumbled around her, that perfect lopsided smile that could break a man's heart at fifty paces on her face.

His beautiful, graceful, witty Layla. The woman

who'd entered this cold, palatial villa and filled it with warmth. Filled *him* with warmth.

The woman rejected before her birth by the father who should have loved and protected her. Rejected by the grandparents who should have loved and protected her too.

And now rejected by him.

God help him, he'd pushed her away. Cruelly. On top of all the other wrongs he'd done to the woman who'd dedicated her life to helping those unable to help themselves. A woman who refused to seek vengeance for fear of creating new victims from it.

A shining angel of light in a cold, dark world.

He'd pushed her away.

The image before his eyes vanished.

The pain that ripped through him was enough to bring him to his knees.

Layla exited the underground and trudged carefully through the sleet falling around her and landing like slush, and was thankful of the small mercy of having enough money in the bank to pay for decent winter boots. Thankful that her mum had a decent coat and set of boots to protect her from the elements too. Thankful for her mum full stop. It was hard to fall deep into despair when you had such unflinching love and support.

That didn't stop her heart feeling bleaker than the weather or stop her eyes from leaking. A weekend of comedy films and she'd cried silently through all of them, smiling only during the times her baby woke up to play football in her belly, then crying again to know Sebastiano wasn't there to share it with her.

She couldn't stop thinking about him and thinking about that awful, awful evening when everything had fallen apart. His ashen face at her home truths. The guilt she felt for going behind his back and buying the house even after she'd agreed not to. She hadn't made a verbal promise not to but the implication had been there.

So deeply was Sebastiano on her mind that when she walked into the skyscraper's lobby and stamped the sludge off her boots, it was no surprise that her gaze zoomed straight to his photo before she had the chance to block it.

Lowering her stare, she passed through the usual security checks and turned in the direction of the elevators. A waft of his cologne almost made her stumble but she kept walking, and—

'Layla.'

Her heart stopped before her feet did.

It took for ever to find the courage to turn around.

It was him. Standing close enough that if she reached an arm out she'd be able to touch him.

Her heart kick-started back to life and suddenly she was clinging tightly to the large bag slung over her shoulder and struggling to breathe.

She *should* have foreseen this, she realised dimly through the blood rushing in her head. With the size of the building and the infrequency of his visits to it, there had only been a slim chance of their paths crossing here, but she should have prepared herself. After all, she knew better than anyone that the tiniest of odds could play out. Her baby was proof of that.

It had never taken so much to say two words. 'Hello, Sebastiano.'

His chest rose. It hurt to see it. It hurt to see him. Hurt

to see how just eight days apart from him had distorted her memories. She didn't remember his face being so gaunt or so…pallid. Or his eyes being bloodshot.

'Can we talk?'

She gaped at him. It was hard to be certain if she'd heard him correctly through the roar in her head. She didn't remember his voice being so hoarse.

He closed his eyes and bowed his head. 'That's fair. After the way things were left between us I don't blame you for not wanting to talk to me.'

Had she said that?

'I will make it quick.' The tiniest quirk of his lips that was in no way a smile. 'I know you need to start work. I'm sorry for doing it here but I only landed an hour ago and I knew you would have left home and I would be more likely to catch you here in the lobby than anywhere else.'

Alone in the empty dressing room, everything had become clear. Hours and hours Sebastiano had sat on the hard floor, paralysed, the depths of what he'd done pounding into him. And then his loss had hit him and all the pain he'd been feeling up to that point was nothing, nothing, compared to the agony that had ripped through him.

He'd lost Layla.

But she'd never been his to lose.

Gasping for air, he'd groped for his phone. He'd called his lawyer, and then he'd called his PA. 'Get me to London,' he'd whispered to her, hardly aware that it was two in the morning.

Layla clutched her bag even tighter. She had a vague awareness of people swarming around them, hurrying to their offices, busying themselves for the start of another busy working week, all of them oblivious that her heart was smashing so loudly it had woken her sleeping baby.

He lifted a foot as if to move closer then hesitated. 'Layla…' Something that looked much like pain flashed over his beautiful face. 'I know an apology can't make up for what I've done to you but I have to try. I have to try because you deserve it. I'm…' He shook his head and ran his fingers through his ungroomed hair. 'I'm everything you said I am, and more. I am an arrogant, self-absorbed bastard. But you didn't get everything right. I didn't cut you off and ghost you because you were a bar tender but because the way you made me feel terrified the hell out of me. What I feel for you is like nothing on this earth. That magic was there from the start and I felt it as deeply as you did but I'm a coward. I don't know if it would have been different if I'd known who you really were.' Another quirk of the lips that wasn't a smile. 'I think what I felt for you would have made me run whatever I believed you to be. All those months working so hard not to think about you stopped me thinking altogether. That's the power you had over me even then. I didn't pay attention to the things that matter as much as I should have and the result…the loss of a billion euros.'

He pinched the bridge of his nose before continuing. 'I avoided the club for months until I thought it was safe to return. I thought you'd be gone. It wasn't even a conscious choice. But I couldn't run from you the second time. What you did that night—I fully deserved it. The way I cut you off was unforgivable—but it brought me to life. Everything I'd been suppressing, all the feelings I'd been hiding from, it all hit me.' He shook his head. 'I didn't know a force like that was possible. It shook my heart…shook all of me. I was obsessed by you. Unhealthily obsessed. And I schemed and plotted to make you mine and force you into my life, all the while telling myself that it was what you deserved, what you owed me.' He let out a disbelieving laugh and shook his head. 'Can you believe I told myself that *you* owed *me*? You don't owe me anything, Layla. You never did. You certainly don't owe me your trust and that's what it comes down to, isn't it? I love you and I think a part of you loves me too—or maybe that's my arrogance rearing up again— but there is no trust. I killed it when I deleted your number from my phone and everything I have done since has only proved that you were right not to trust me. I'm not surprised you went to such lengths to protect yourself. I'm only surprised that you can bear to look at me. But know this—I will go to my grave regretting my treatment of you.'

She wiped away the tears blinding her and saw the contortion of his face.

'I'm sorry for everything, Layla. And I pray that one day you can find it in your heart to forgive me.' Swallowing, he reached into his inside coat pocket. 'These are divorce papers. I've already signed my part and postdated it—we have to wait a year to lodge it but I wanted you to have this now so that you can sleep knowing your freedom is in your hands, and not in mine.'

She stared from the envelope in his hand back to his face and whispered, 'You're letting me go?'

Tears swam in his eyes. His voice was hoarse when he said, 'You were never mine to keep. Love without freedom is no love and I cannot endure another day knowing I've clipped the wings of so beautiful a spirit and tethered her to me. All I ask is that I be involved in our child's life—I do want to be a father to it.'

'Of course,' she said dazedly. 'You can be as involved as much as you want to be.'

He gave a pained laugh. 'I knew you'd say that. It's so much more than I deserve.'

'It's what our child deserves.'

'I knew you'd say that too. It's what you deserved from your father and I wish like hell that I could travel back in time and force him to meet you. If he had done...' He swallowed. 'There is not a soul on this earth who could resist falling in love with you.' And then his gaze dropped down to her belly and he sighed. 'You will keep me updated?'

'I promise.'

Another pained laugh before he put his fingers to his lips, kissed them and then pressed them against Layla's mouth. 'Goodbye, Layla.'

And then he turned around and walked away, and the swarm of workers continued to stream around her, only a few giving double takes at the tears streaming down her face.

CHAPTER FOURTEEN

LAYLA STEPPED OUT of the elevator with no memory of stepping into it.

The envelope was still clutched in her hand.

Not moving beyond the threshold, she stared around at the vast reception area where two nail-biting women were waiting nervously on the plush chairs, then gazed beyond the reception to the library where paralegals and others were reading legal texts, photocopying documents, chatting amongst themselves, and then turned her stare to the long, wide corridor. The fourth door on the left opened into her office. Like all the other solicitors, she now worked on a computer that was ultra-modern and ultra-speedy.

She gazed back at the two waiting women. They weren't her clients. She knew neither of their stories. Looking more closely, she saw the remnants of a bruise under the eye of the woman to the left. A victim of domestic abuse? Was she here because she'd heard through Clayton Community Law's growing network that this was a place she could get legal help against her abuser for free? Maybe the woman really had just walked into a door. No two people's stories were the same, the only commonality between their clients being they couldn't afford to pay for legal help or the free help they were entitled to wasn't enough for what they needed.

And now they could help more people. A lot more people. They were already looking at premises in three other cities as they sought to expand their services to other areas of the country.

None of this would have been possible without Sebastiano. He'd been under no obligation to do anything more than pay her the money. He'd given the firm this vast floor to work from because he wanted to, and if it had been to salve his conscience as she thought then it meant he *had* a conscience. And if he had a conscience then it meant he was capable of redemption...

'Layla? Are you okay?'

She blinked.

Audrey, one of her colleagues, was staring at her with concern.

Layla stepped back, her head alternating between nodding and shaking. 'I need to go. I'm sorry.'

Holding her belly, she walked as fast as her heavily pregnant body would carry her to the elevator. Outside the building, she hailed a black cab.

Maybe her mother was right about fate because the sleet had cleared. The Monday morning traffic parted for them and every single traffic light stayed on green.

When the driver pulled up outside the large suburban house on the quiet street, she paid with her phone without even listening to the price.

Inside, music played loudly above her. Holding tightly to the bannister, she climbed the stairs and followed the noise to one of the guest rooms where she found her mum on a step ladder painting the walls a soft yellow, humming along to the music.

Seeing Layla, she stepped off the ladder and hit the off button on the radio. 'What's happened?' she asked anxiously.

'Mum, what did he say to you to get you to move to Sicily? Please tell me.'

The anxiety disappeared.

After the longest time spent just staring at her, her mother sighed and smiled. 'He said that you needed me.'

Layla's heart caught and her hand fluttered to her mouth.

That had been the last thing she'd expected to hear.

What made it more unexpected was that it had been true. Layla had been thrust, pregnant, into a new world and desperately trying to swim in it whilst fighting against her feelings for her own husband. Sebastiano might not have recognised her fears but he'd recognised that she needed her mother when even Layla hadn't recognised she needed her.

He'd known enough about the Sansom mother-daughter relationship, too, to know it was a need her mother would never refuse.

Her mother had only agreed to move from the hellhole because it was what Layla had wanted.

After resting the paintbrush she was holding on the tin, her mother lanced her again with her compassionate stare. 'He isn't your father. You do know that?'

Too choked to speak, Layla nodded.

'Sebastiano loves you.'

She nodded again. He did love her.

And she loved him. Loved him with the same unhealthy obsessiveness that he loved her.

It was a love that had weaved into her veins and tightened its tendrils even as she'd kidded herself that she could guard her heart against him.

A ray of winter sunlight shone through the window and pierced Layla's heart. She closed her eyes and let its warmth fill her, and when she opened them again, it was like opening them for the very first time.

Sebastiano loved her.

'Mum, do you like this house?'

Confusion creased her mother's brow. 'You know I do.'

'More than our old house?'

'Much more.' An impish grin widened her face. 'It is nice to go into a garden and not be overcome with the fumes of cannabis plants when the wind's blowing in the wrong direction.'

Layla burst into laughter. 'I'm glad you said that, because it's yours.' Then she threw her arms around the woman who had sacrificed so much to bring Layla into the world and given her all the love and emotional security a child could wish for.

Holding her tightly, she whispered, 'Thank you for everything. If I can be half as good a mother to my child as you've been to me then I will consider myself to have done a great job, but now it's time to cut the apron strings. No more putting me first. You need to start living for *you*. Go and explore the world. Find yourself a lover. Find yourself two lovers! Whatever you want to do. Just get out there and start living.'

As she pulled apart from the embrace, tears welled in her mother's eyes. 'Oh, honey… I am so proud of you.'

'Everything I am is because of you, so be proud of yourself.'

Her mum pressed a hand to her heart and sniffed as she smiled. 'You're going to him?'

Layla nodded and smiled her first real smile in so very long. 'Yes. I'm going home.'

Home to the man she'd subconsciously found a different form of emotional security with from her very first night in his villa when she'd fallen into a deep, deep sleep.

It was late when Sebastiano returned to the villa.

He'd never felt so drained in his life. He had to force his leaden legs to climb the stairs.

He would sell the place. Find somewhere new. Somewhere Layla's ghost didn't haunt him.

He could smell her perfume, stronger than a memory, as if she'd very recently walked the mezzanine.

It was more than a man could endure.

But endure it he must. For the sake of his child.

Knowing that in a couple of months the life he and Layla had created together would be born was the one spot of brightness in a world that had turned so bleak.

He couldn't even face sleeping in the bed they'd shared together. It didn't matter how many times the sheets were changed—and he was having them changed daily for this very reason—her scent still permeated.

He dragged his legs into his bedroom. Her perfume was even stronger in here. He would brush his teeth and then get his head down in one of the guest rooms…

He came to an abrupt halt.

Closing his eyes, he counted to ten then opened them.

His lungs closed. His throat closed. His heart turned over.

Layla was on his bed.

She was naked. To her side was a pile of shredded paper.

Her left wrist was handcuffed to the bedpost.

Her beautiful forget-me-not eyes were staring at him, an emotion filling them that filled his own eyes with tears he could do nothing to stop.

He didn't feel his legs move towards her.

Overwhelmed with the emotions swirling like a tempest inside him, he sat on the bed and gently placed his hand on her swollen belly. Movement beneath his palm turned his heart over again.

She smiled tremulously and nodded.

Wiping away a falling tear, he kissed the swell, right where his child had moved, and then reached for the tiny key she'd thrown out of her reach and unlocked the cuffs, pressing his lips to the delicate skin it had been wrapped around.

She gave another tremulous smile and palmed his cheek. 'I love you, Sebastiano Russo,' she said quietly, her forget-me-not eyes brimming with emotion. 'With every fibre of my being. I love you and I *do* trust you.'

He sucked in a breath, hardly daring to believe what she was saying.

She smiled and kissed him gently. 'You're like a wounded animal when hurt but you never lie...except to yourself...and for all the wrongs you did after our night together and in the way you forced me to marry you, you always, *always* treated me with respect.' She kissed him again then stared deep into his eyes. 'You're like a wounded animal when you're hurt but I'm like one when I'm scared. The house was never about you, it was about *me* because I was too scared and you were too stubborn to admit the truth—that I belong to you and you belong to me and our baby belongs to us both until they're old enough to belong to themselves.'

Overwhelmed, Sebastiano nuzzled his cheek against hers and breathed in the scent of Layla's skin, still hardly daring to believe that he would spend the rest of his life breathing it.

Her hand cupped the back of his neck. Her nose rubbing into his temple, she whispered, 'I'm not scared any more.'

And neither was he, Sebastiano thought dazedly as their mouths crushed together and their arms wrapped tightly around each other, and the light and warmth that came from the sexy angelic creature who loved him— Layla *loved* him!—seeped into his cold heart and brought him back to life.

It was a warmth that would fuel him for the rest of his life.

EPILOGUE

EXCLUSIVE!

Sicilian billionaire banker Sebastiano Russo and his wife, English lawyer Layla Russo, have welcomed another baby into the world!

CMB can exclusively report that the Russos, famed for their philanthropy and the hosting of parties with guest lists to make A-list celebrities weep, have added to their growing brood with a healthy baby boy. No name has yet been decided for the child, who is brother to Jilly (six), Lara (five) and Dante (two). But if tradition is anything to go by, CMB's money is on it being an Italian name!

More to follow as it comes...

* * * * *